DreamWorks

PENGUINS
of MADAGASCAR

VOLUME ONE: WHEN IN ROME

THIS BOOK IS BROUGHT TO YOU BY...

Senior Editor Martin Eden
Production Manager Obi Onoura
Production Supervisors Jackie Flook, Maria Pearson
Production Assistant Peter James
Studio Manager Emma Smith
Circulation Manager Steve Tothill
Marketing Manager Ricky Claydon
Publishing Manager Darryl Tothill
Publishing Director Chris Teather
Operations Director Leigh Baulch
Executive Director Vivian Cheung
Publisher Nick Landau

ISBN: 9781782762515

The Penguins of Madagascar © 2015 DreamWorks Animation L. L. C. No part of this publication may be reproduced, stored in a retrieval system, or transmitted, in any form or by any means, without the prior written permission of the publisher. Names, characters, places and incidents featured in this publication are either the product of the author's imagination or used fictitiously. Any resemblance to actual persons, living or dead (except for satirical purposes), is entirely coincidental.

10 9 8 7 6 5 4 3 2 1

First printed in China in May 2015.
A CIP catalogue record for this title is available from the British Library.
TCN: 0557

Special thanks to Corinne Combs, Alyssa Mauney, Barbara Layman.

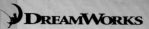

PENGUINS
OF MADAGASCAR

Inside 3 COMIC Strips

THE GREAT DRAIN ROBBERY

WHEN IN ROME

NIGHT OUT

Plus puzzles, profiles, pin-ups, and more!

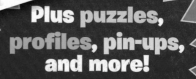

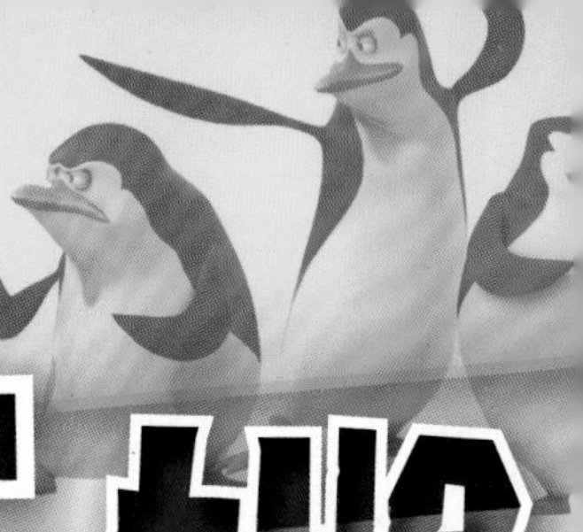

Meet the

Just what makes Skipper and the other penguins tick? Find out more about your favorite flippered characters in our tell-all guide!

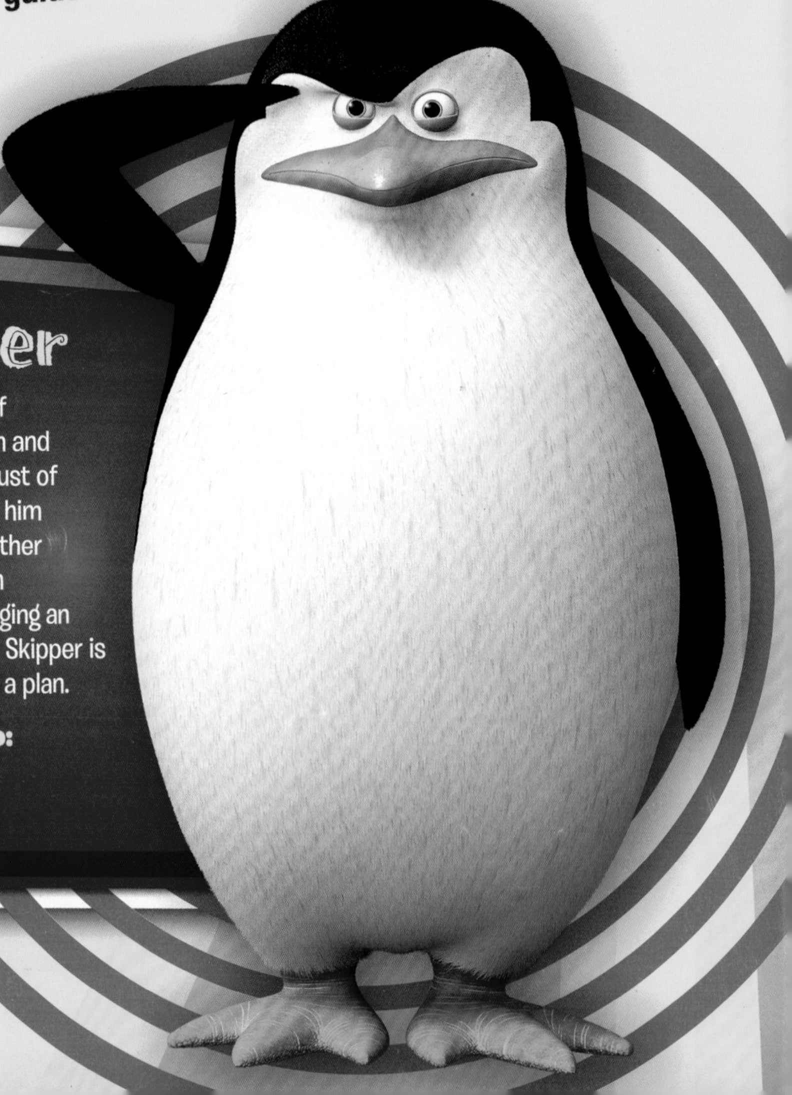

Skipper

He's the leader of the penguin team and he has got the trust of everyone around him (just about). Whether he's tangling with octopi or challenging an undercover wolf, Skipper is the penguin with a plan.

Most likely to:
Motivate you

GANG!

PART 1

Kowalski

The options guy, Skipper's right-hand man. When the team needs to make a move or change course, Kowalski will calculate a way to make it happen!

Most likely to: Escape from any situation!

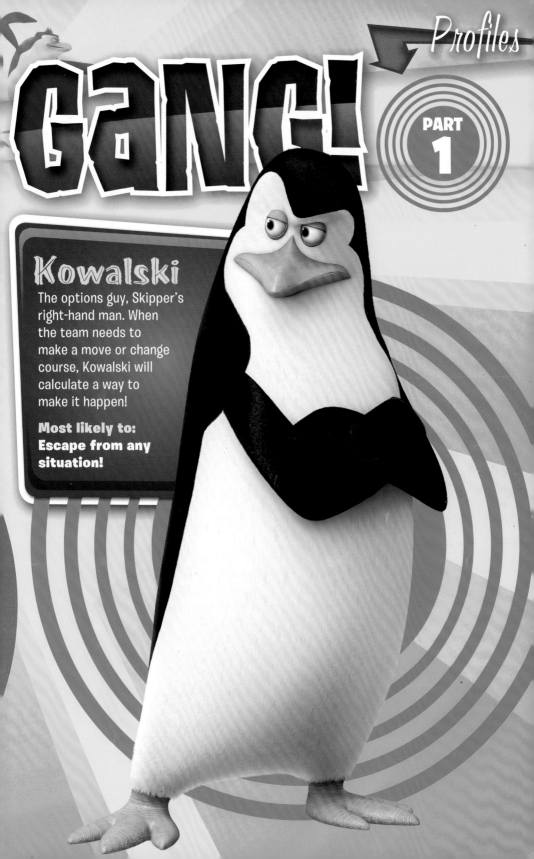

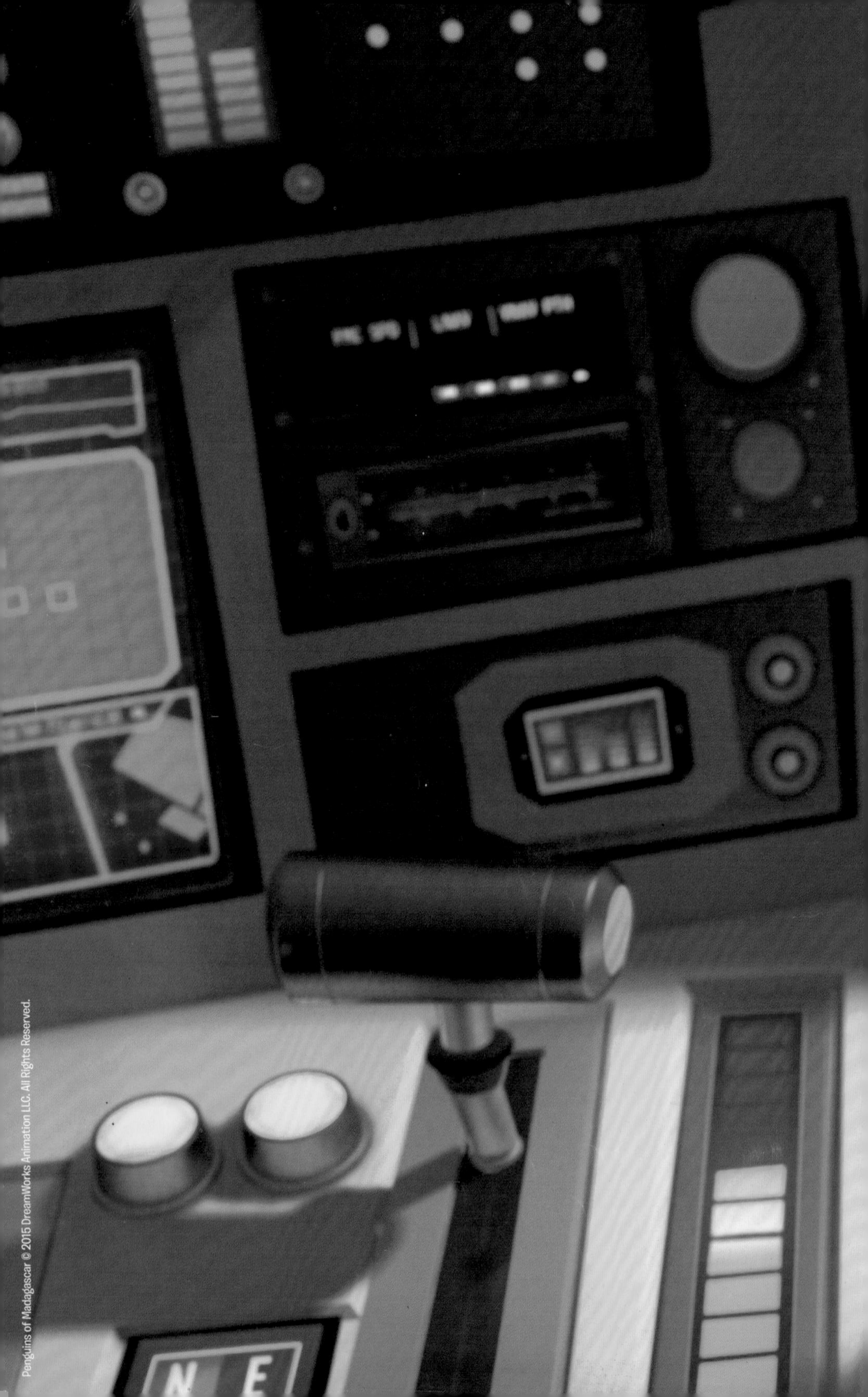

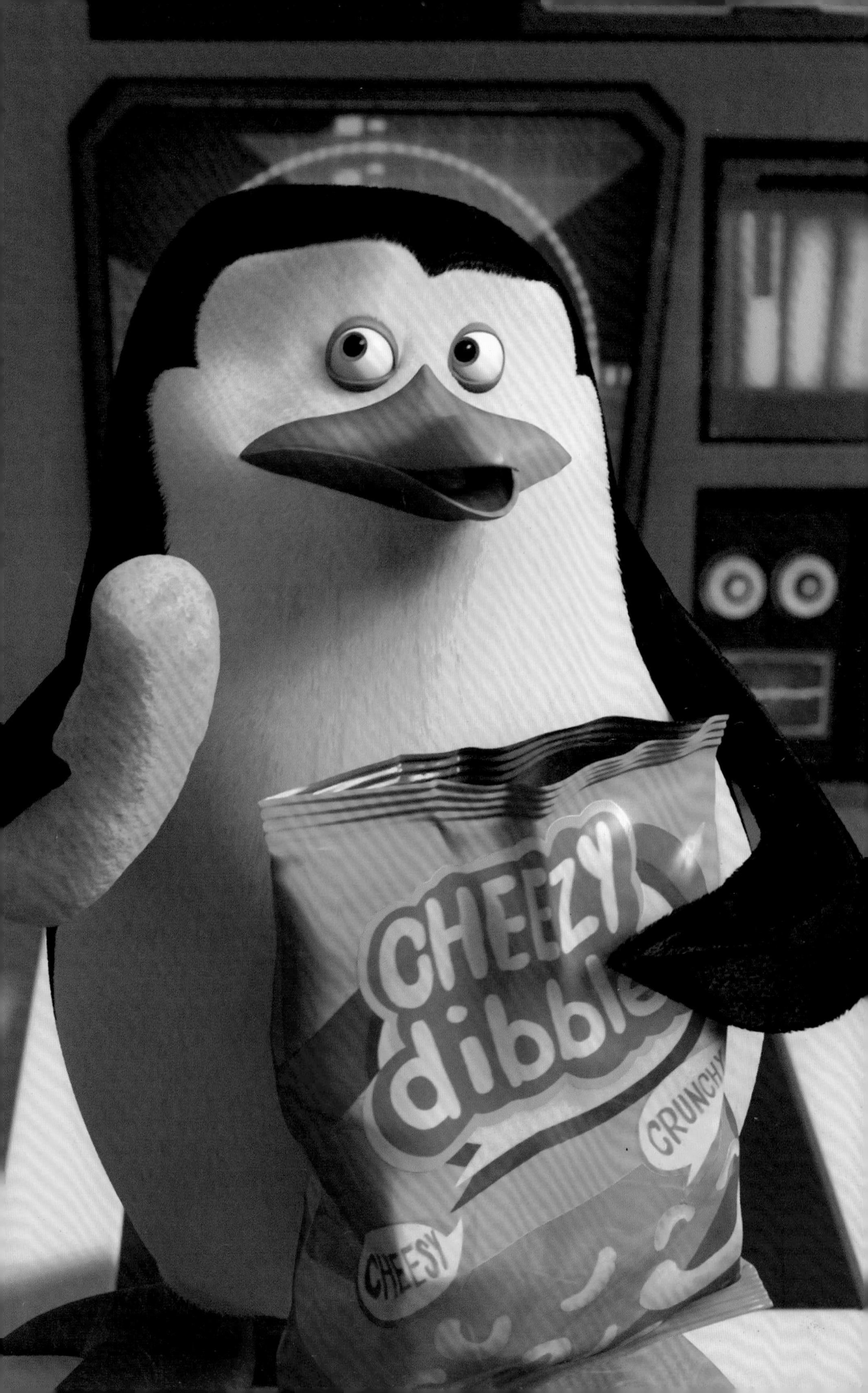
CHEEZY
dibble
CRUNCHY
CHEESY

THE GREAT DRAIN ROBBERY

SCRIPT
Jai Nitz

ART
Lawrence Etherington

LETTERING
Jimmy Betancourt/
Comicraft

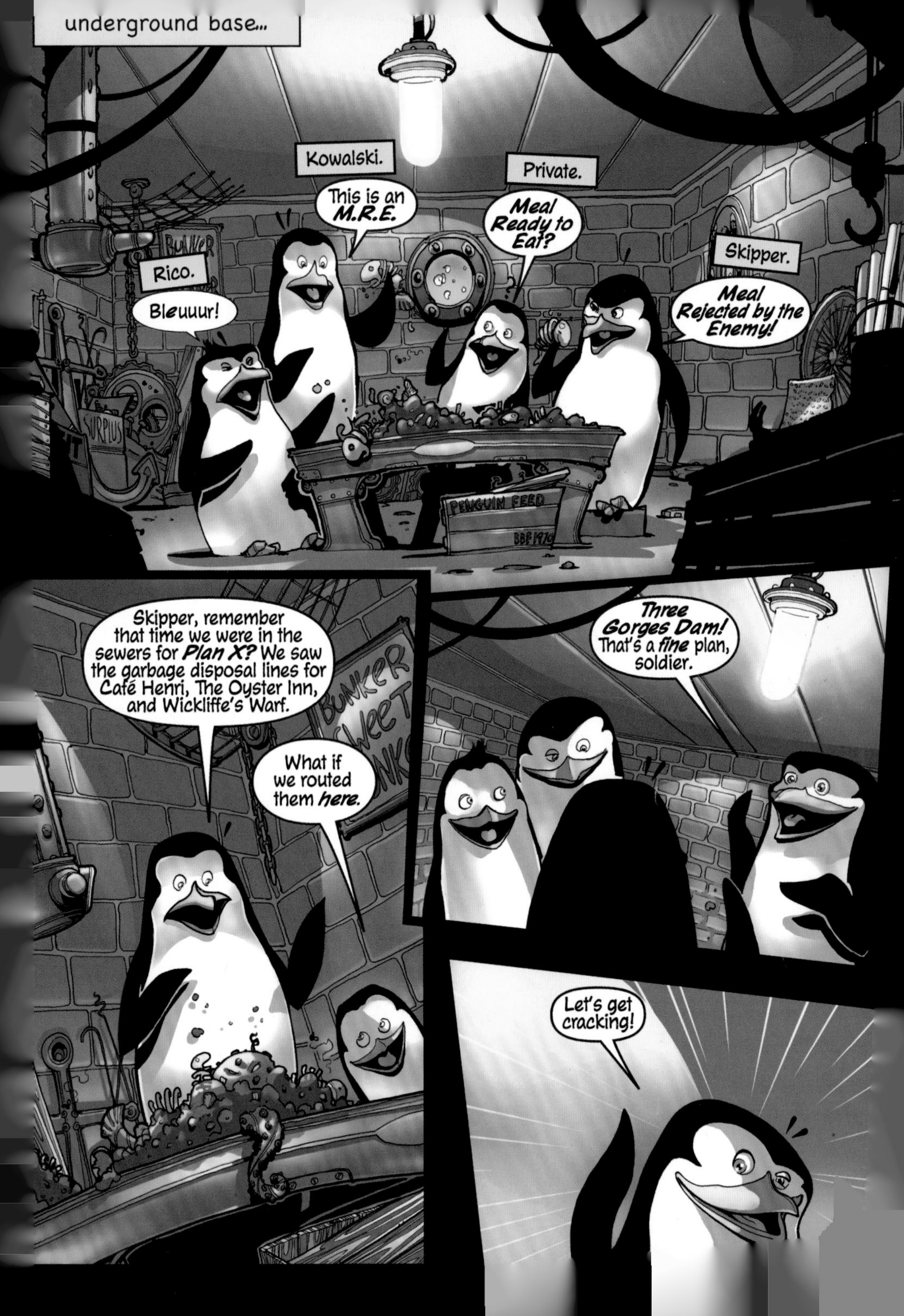

underground base...
Kowalski.
This is an M.R.E.
Private.
Meal Ready to Eat?
Rico.
Bleuuur!
Skipper.
Meal Rejected by the Enemy!
BUNKER
SURPLUS
PENGUIN FEED
BBF 1970
Skipper, remember that time we were in the sewers for *Plan X?* We saw the garbage disposal lines for Café Henri, The Oyster Inn, and Wickliffe's Warf.
What if we routed them *here*.
Three Gorges Dam! That's a *fine* plan, soldier.
Let's get cracking!

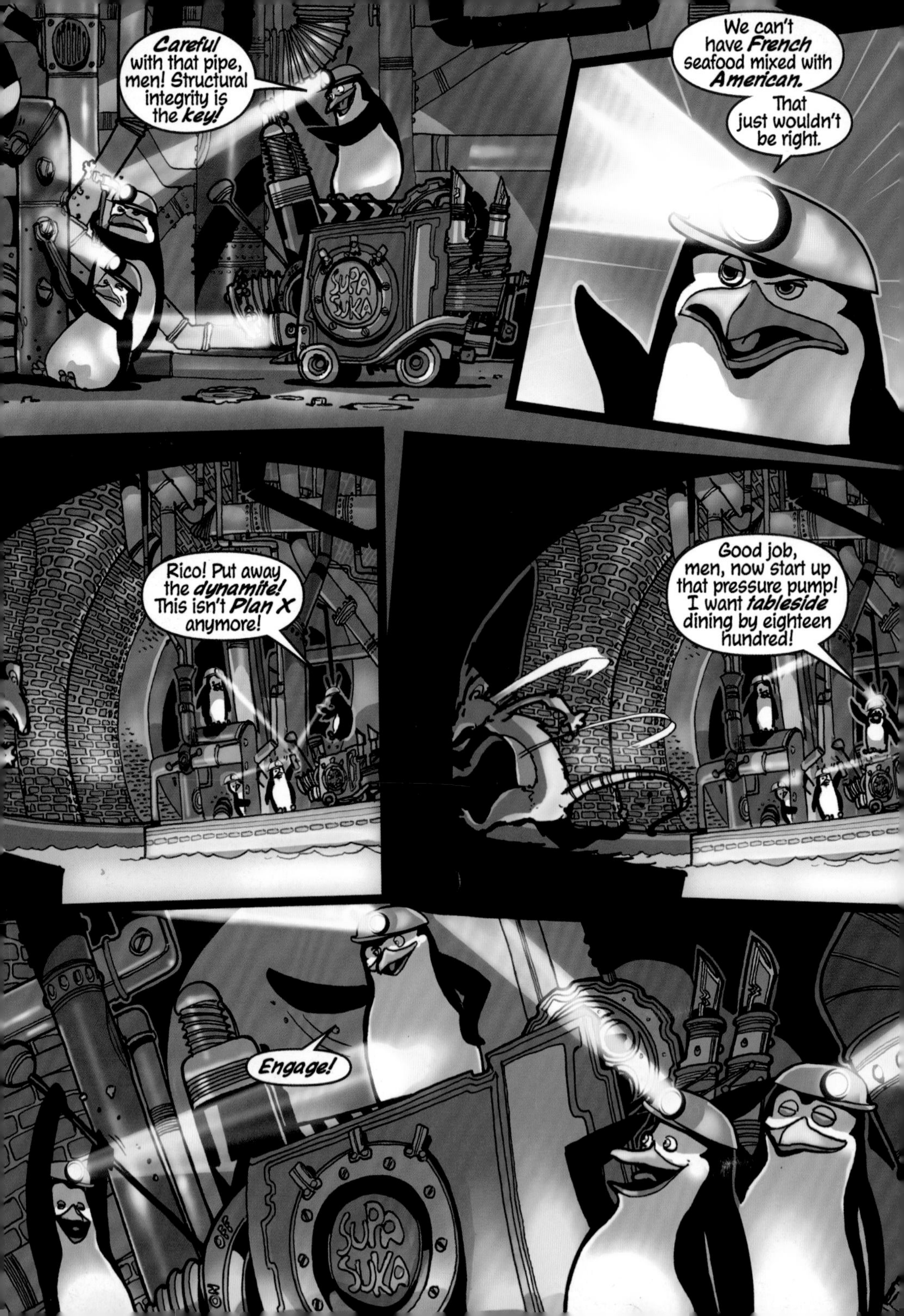
Careful with that pipe, men! Structural integrity is the key!
We can't have French seafood mixed with American.
That just wouldn't be right.
SUPA SUKA
Rico! Put away the dynamite! This isn't Plan X anymore!
Good job, men, now start up that pressure pump! I want tableside dining by eighteen hundred!
Engage!
SUPA SUKA

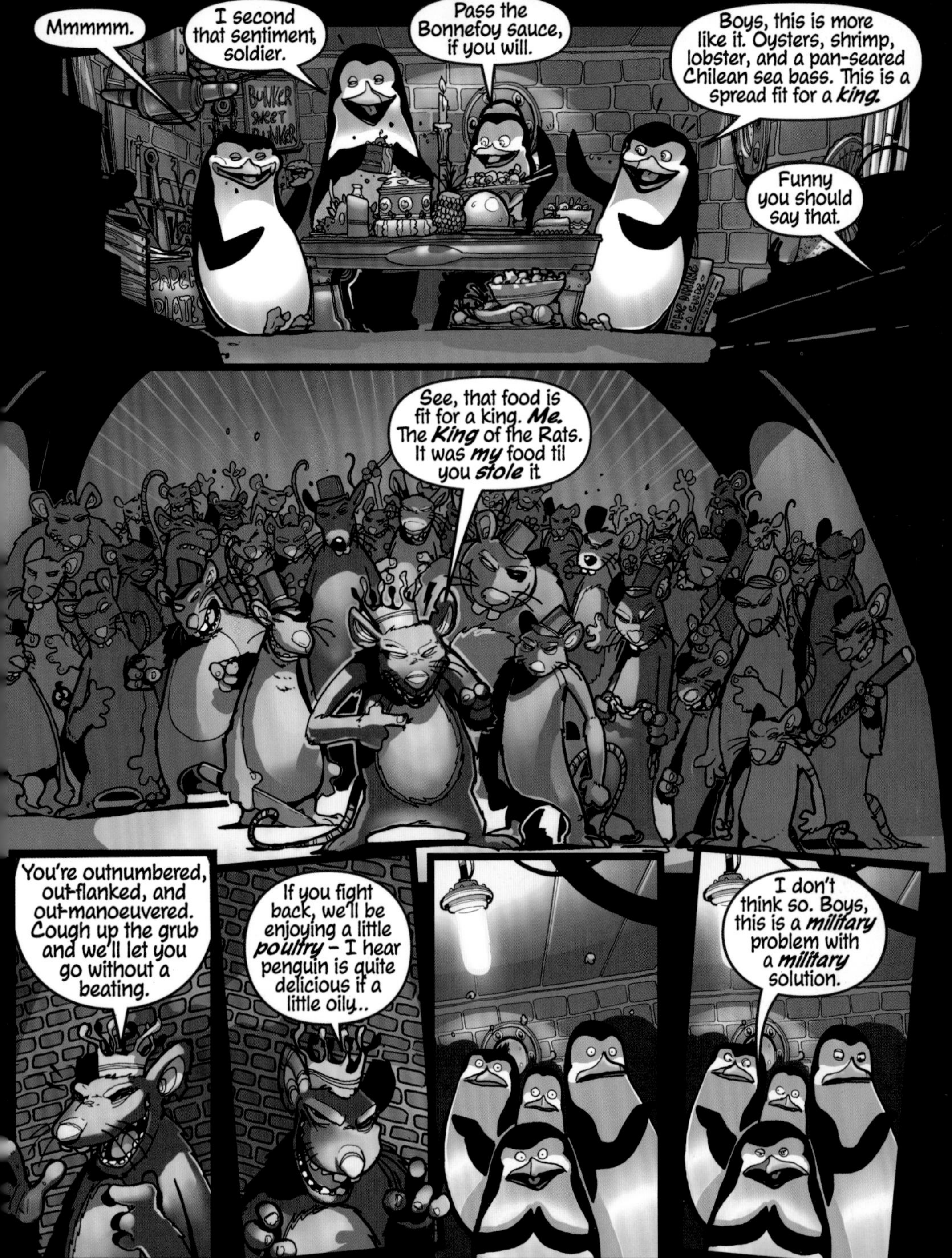

Mmmmm.
I second that sentiment, soldier.
Pass the Bonnefoy sauce, if you will.
Boys, this is more like it. Oysters, shrimp, lobster, and a pan-seared Chilean sea bass. This is a spread fit for a *king.*
Funny you should say that.
BUNKER SWEET BUNKER
PAPER PLATES
See, that food is fit for a king. *Me.* The *King* of the Rats. It was *my* food til you *stole* it
You're outnumbered, out-flanked, and out-manoeuvered. Cough up the grub and we'll let you go without a beating.
If you fight back, we'll be enjoying a little *poultry* – I hear penguin is quite delicious if a little oily..
I don't think so. Boys, this is a *military* problem with a *military* solution.

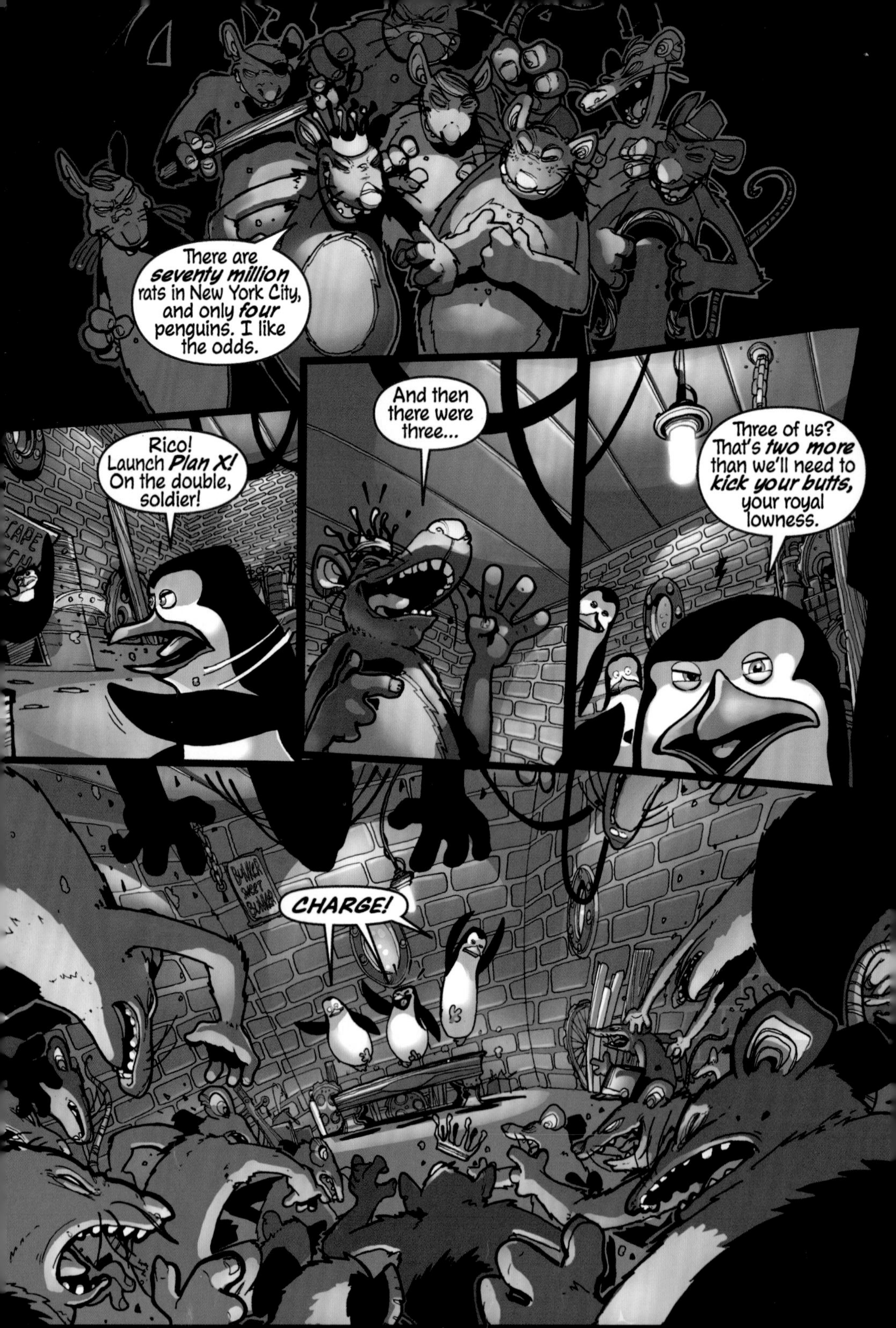
There are **seventy million** rats in New York City, and only **four** penguins. I like the odds.
Rico! Launch ***Plan X!*** On the double, soldier!
And then there were three...
Three of us? That's ***two more*** than we'll need to ***kick your butts,*** your royal lowness.
CHARGE!

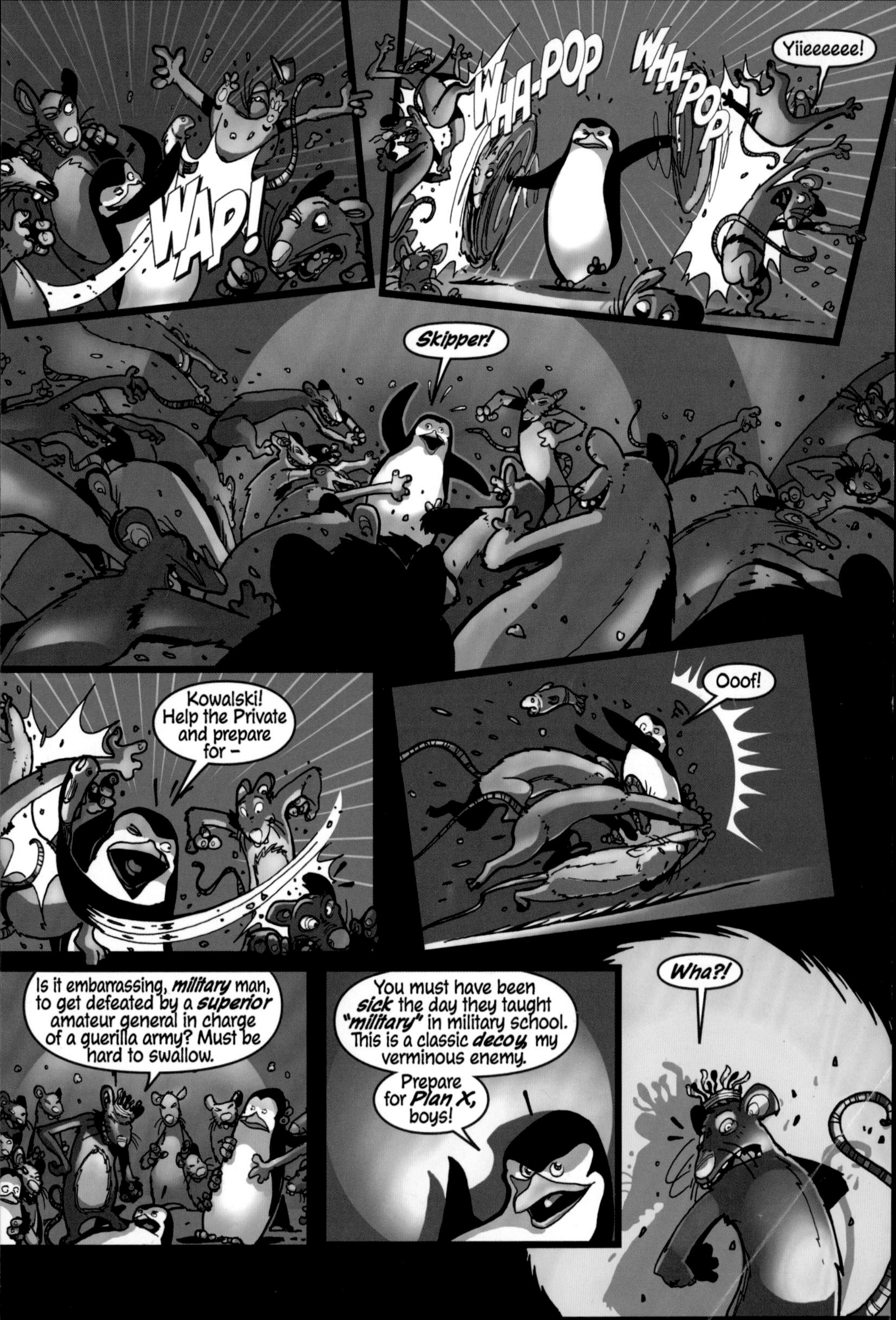
WAP!
WHA-POP
WHA-POP
Yiieeeeee!
Skipper!
Kowalski! Help the Private and prepare for –
Ooof!
Is it embarrassing, military man, to get defeated by a superior amateur general in charge of a guerilla army? Must be hard to swallow.
You must have been sick the day they taught "military" in military school. This is a classic decoy, my verminous enemy.
Prepare for Plan X, boys!
Wha?!

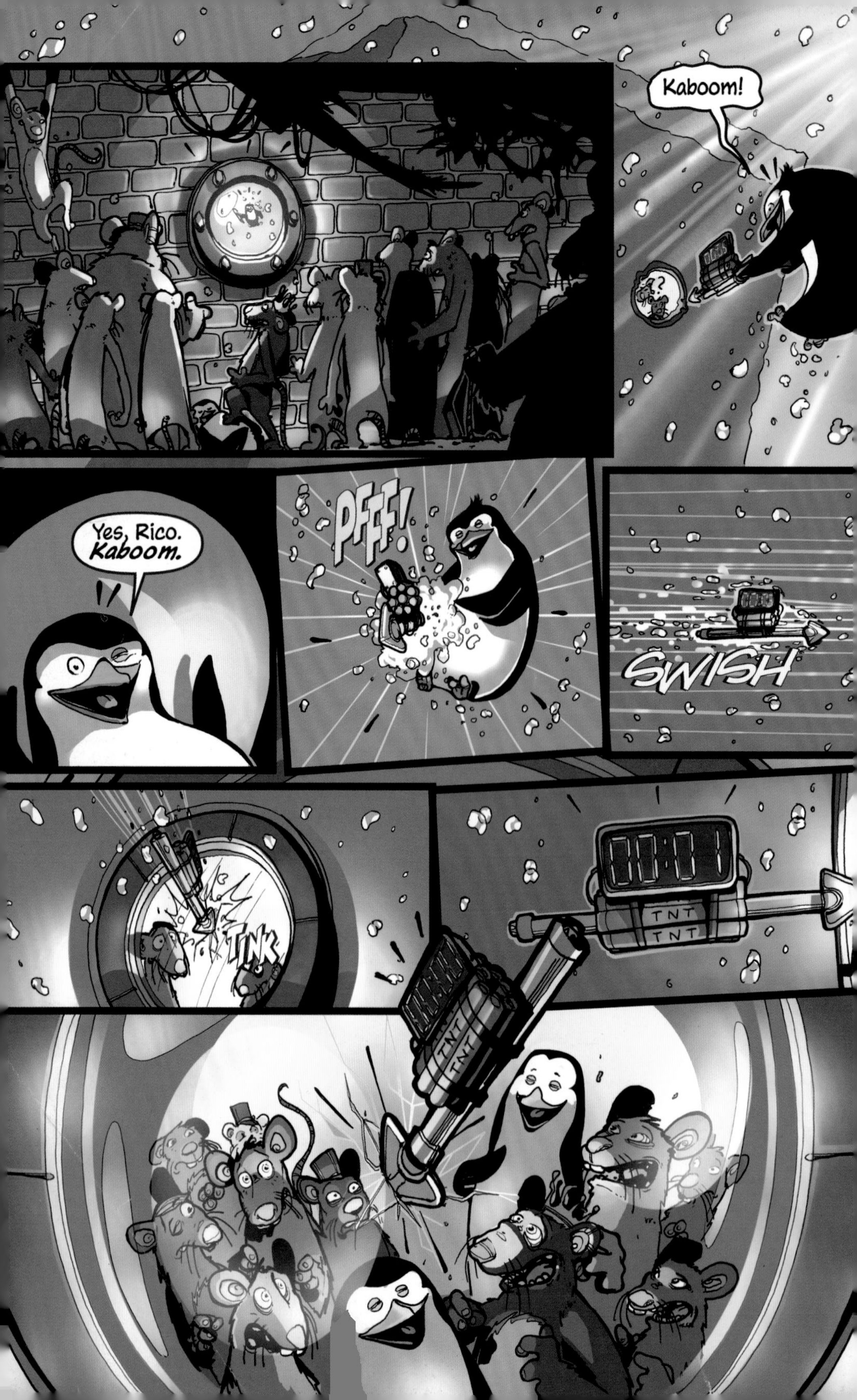
Kaboom!
Yes, Rico.
Kaboom.
PFFF!
SWISH
TINK
TNT
TNT
TNT
TNT

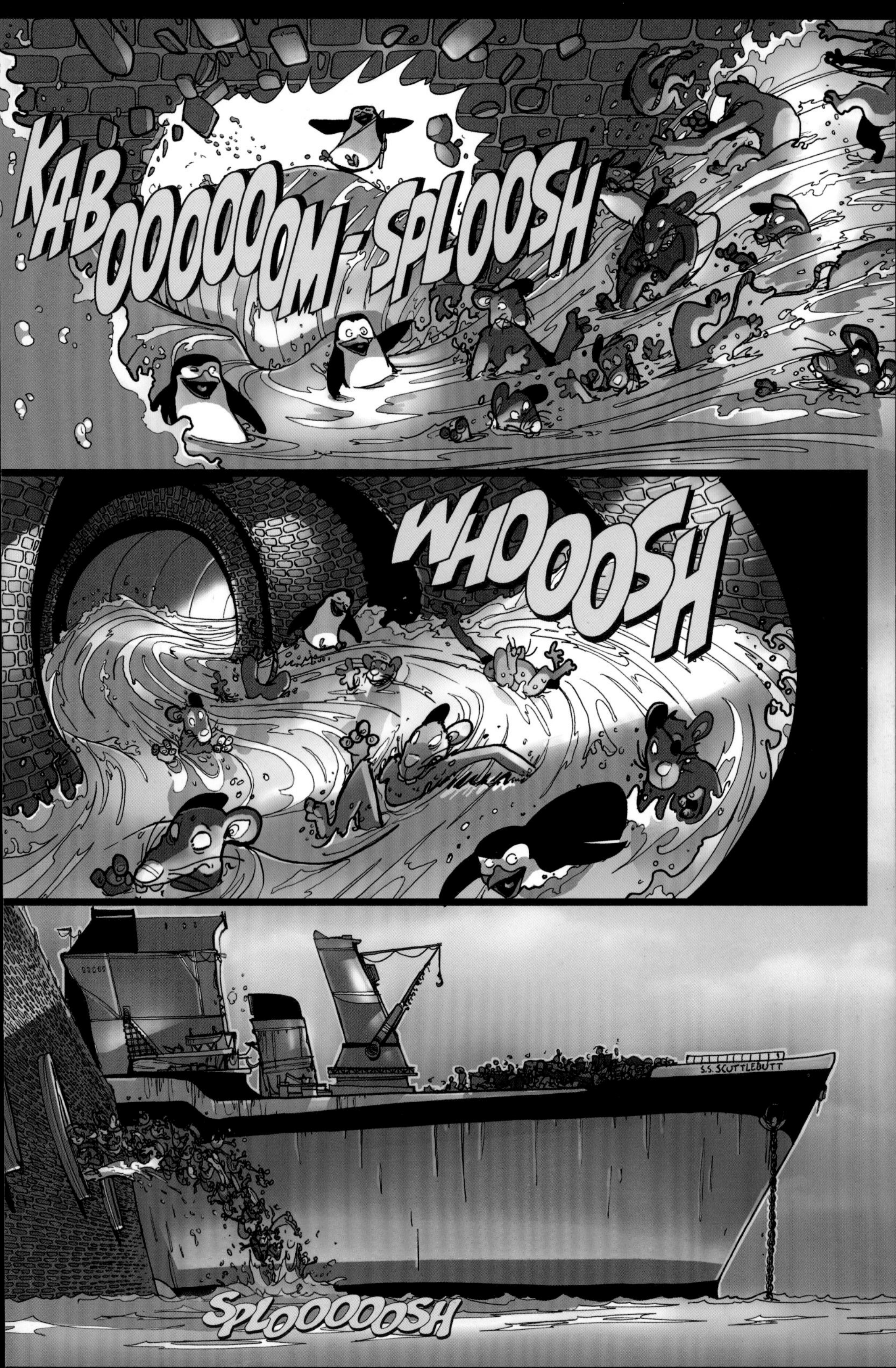
KA-BOOOOOOOM! SPLOOSH
WHOOOSH
S.S. SCUTTLEBUTT
SPLOOOOOOSH

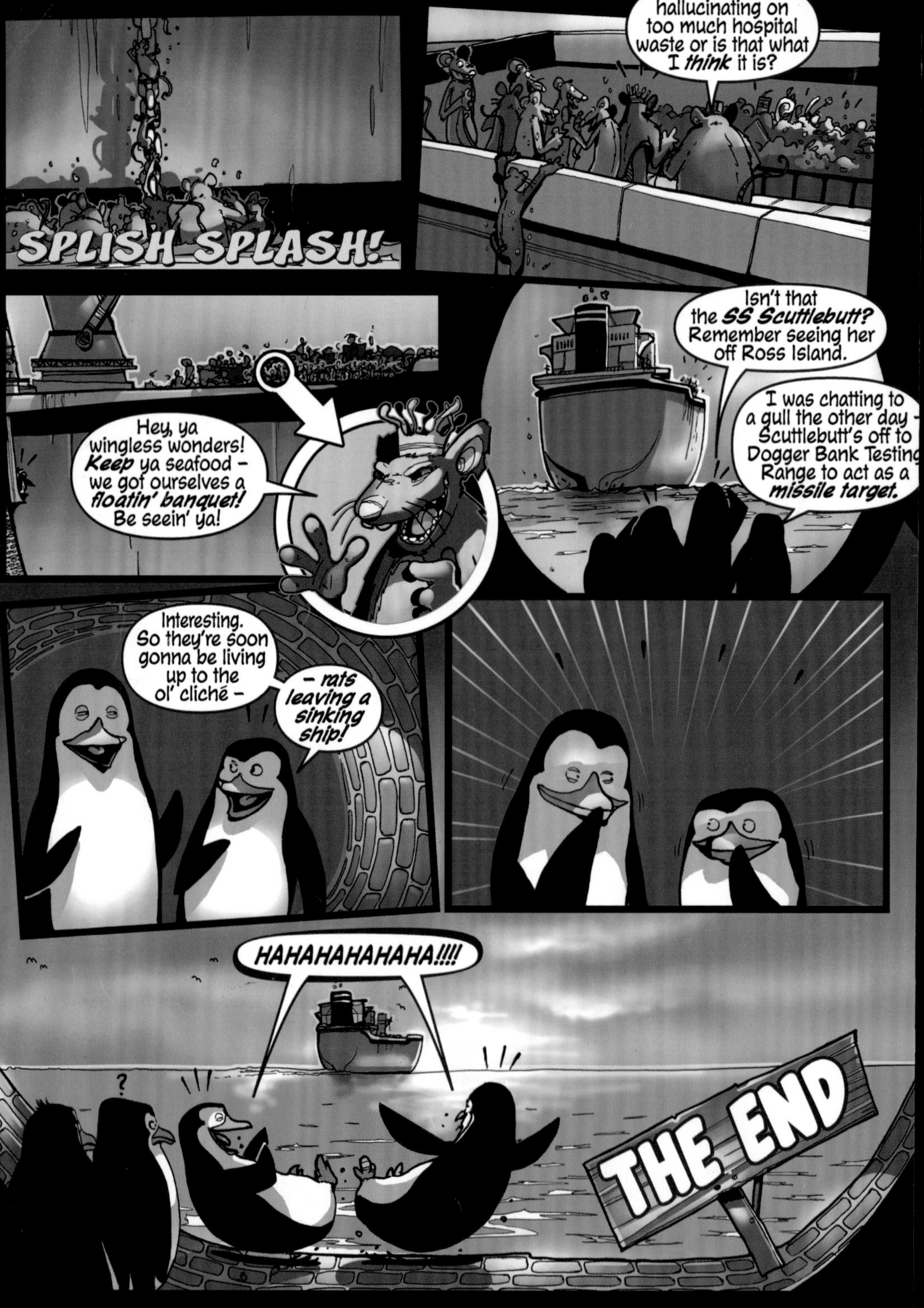
SPLISH SPLASH!
Am I hallucinating on too much hospital waste or is that what I *think* it is?
Hey, ya wingless wonders! ***Keep*** ya seafood – we got ourselves a ***floatin' banquet!*** Be seein' ya!
Isn't that the ***SS Scuttlebutt?*** Remember seeing her off Ross Island.
I was chatting to a gull the other day – Scuttlebutt's off to Dogger Bank Testing Range to act as a ***missile target.***
Interesting. So they're soon gonna be living up to the ol' cliché –
– rats leaving a sinking ship!
HAHAHAHAHAHA!!!!
?
THE END

Game

Spot the Difference

There are 6 differences between these two pictures. Can you find them?

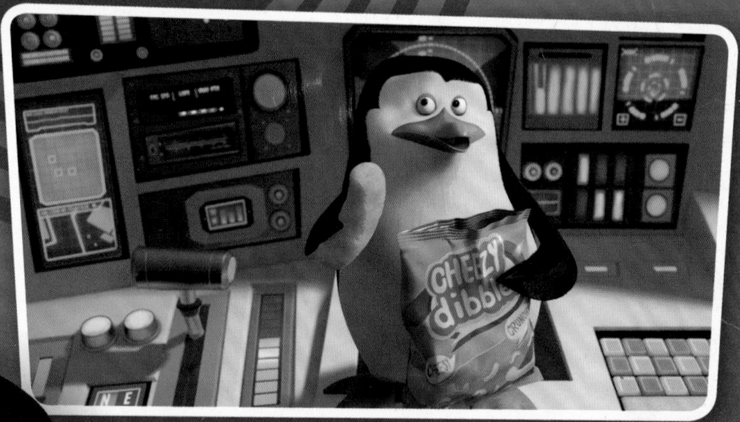
CHEEZY
N E

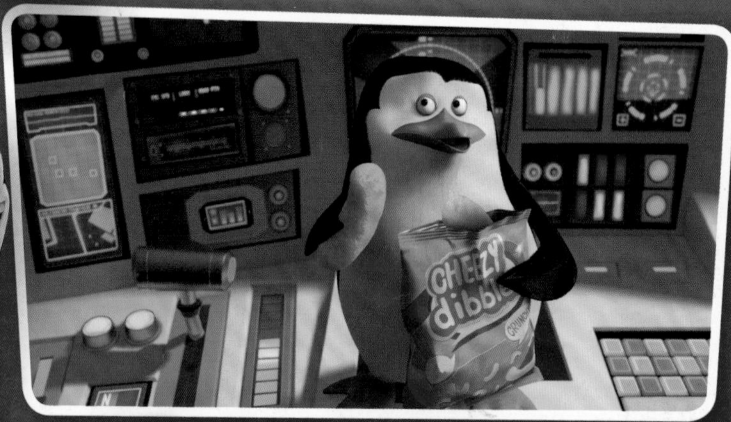
CHEEZY
N

Penguin Funnies

Q: Why don't penguins like classical music?

A: They only like Sole!

Q: Why don't penguins live in Britain?

A: Because they're scared of Wales.

Q: What do you call a penguin in the desert?

A: Lost.

Answers: 1. A little blue square appears on the big blue square on the left; 2. An 'E' is missing, bottom left; 3. Part of the handle on the lower left goes green; 4. A Cheezy Dibble appears at the top of the packet; 5. Some words on the Cheezy Dibbles packet go missing; 6. A blue button near the middle turns red.

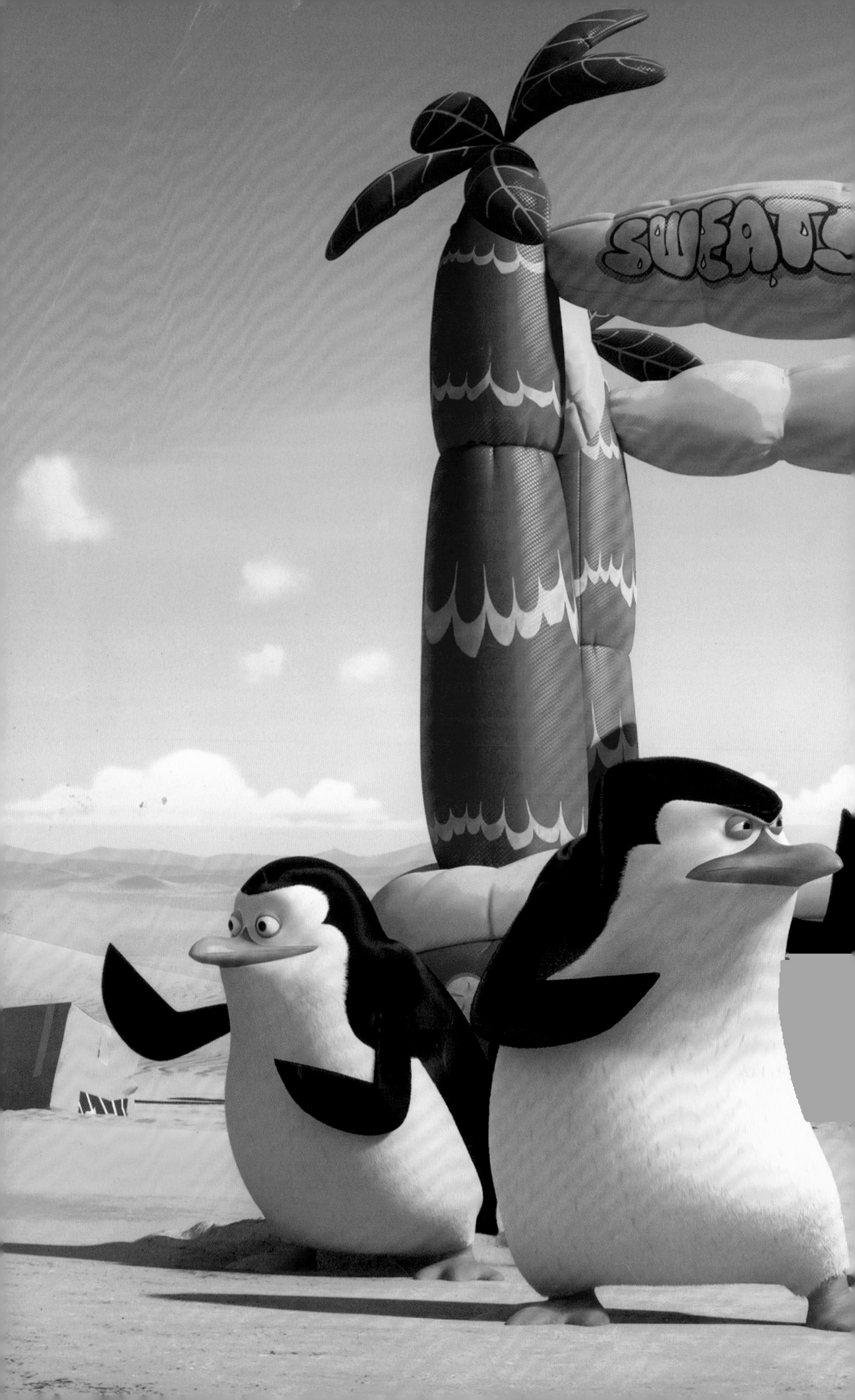

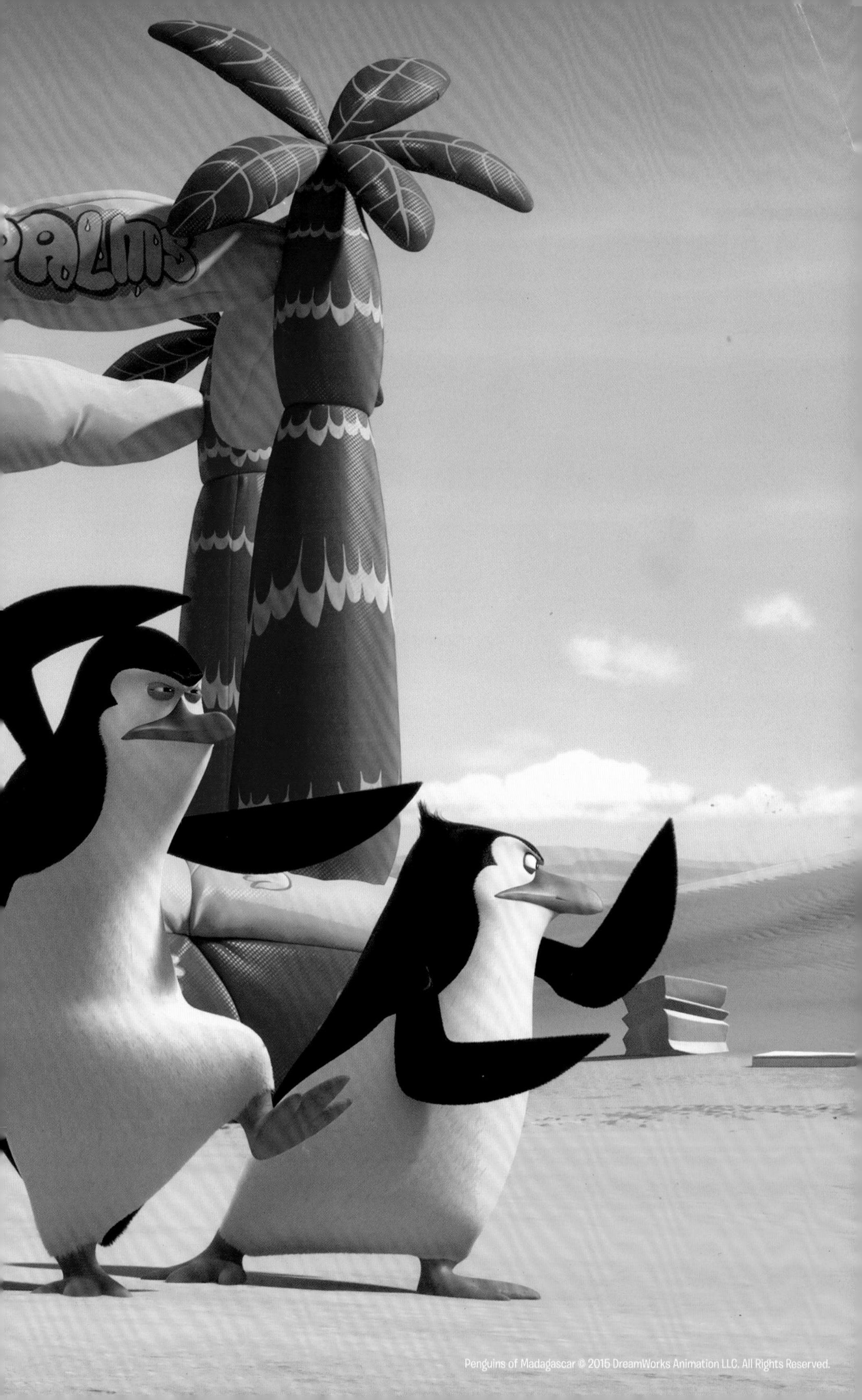

Meet the

Rico

The quiet one of the group, Rico certainly makes up for his lack of speech with his ability to vomit even the most obscure of objects. Crowbar? Check. Chainsaw? Check. Unexploded bomb? Check.

Most likely to: Get you out of a tight fix!

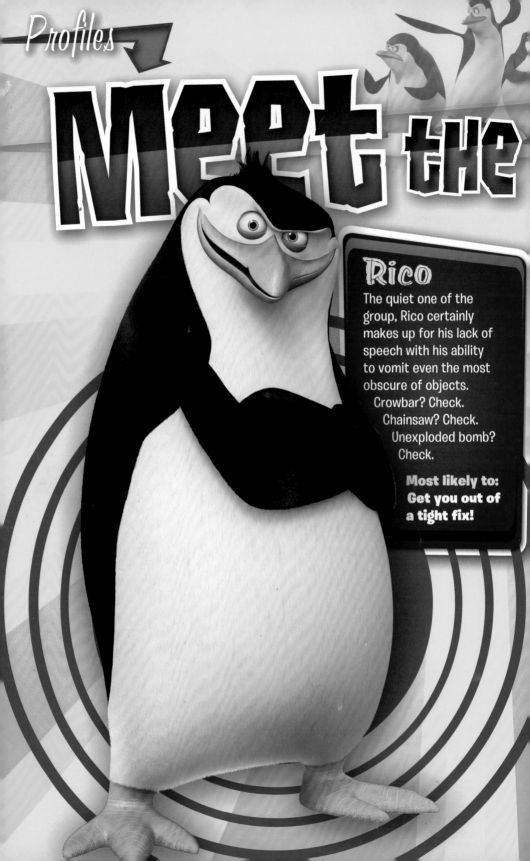

GANG!

PART 2

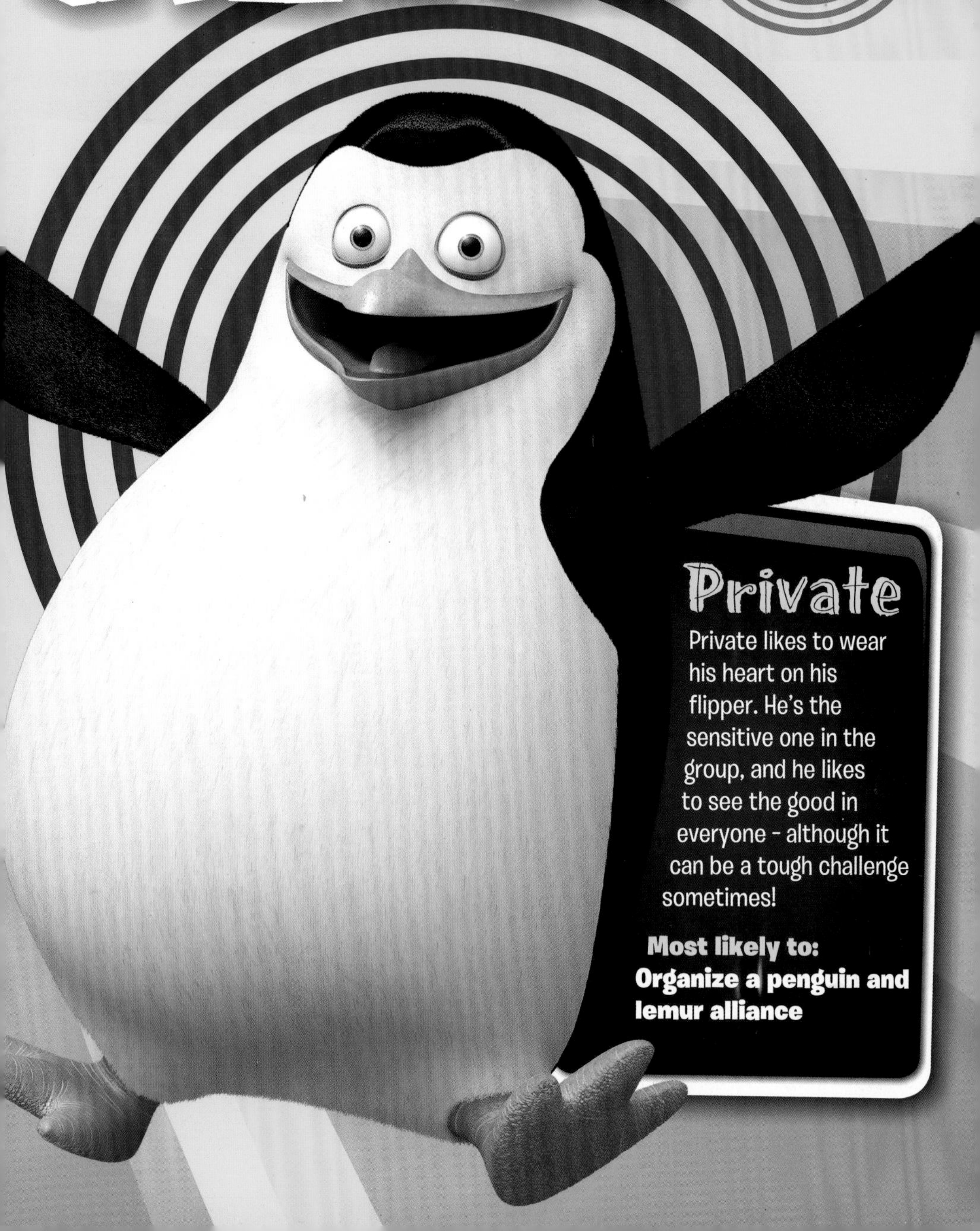

Private

Private likes to wear his heart on his flipper. He's the sensitive one in the group, and he likes to see the good in everyone - although it can be a tough challenge sometimes!

Most likely to:
Organize a penguin and lemur alliance

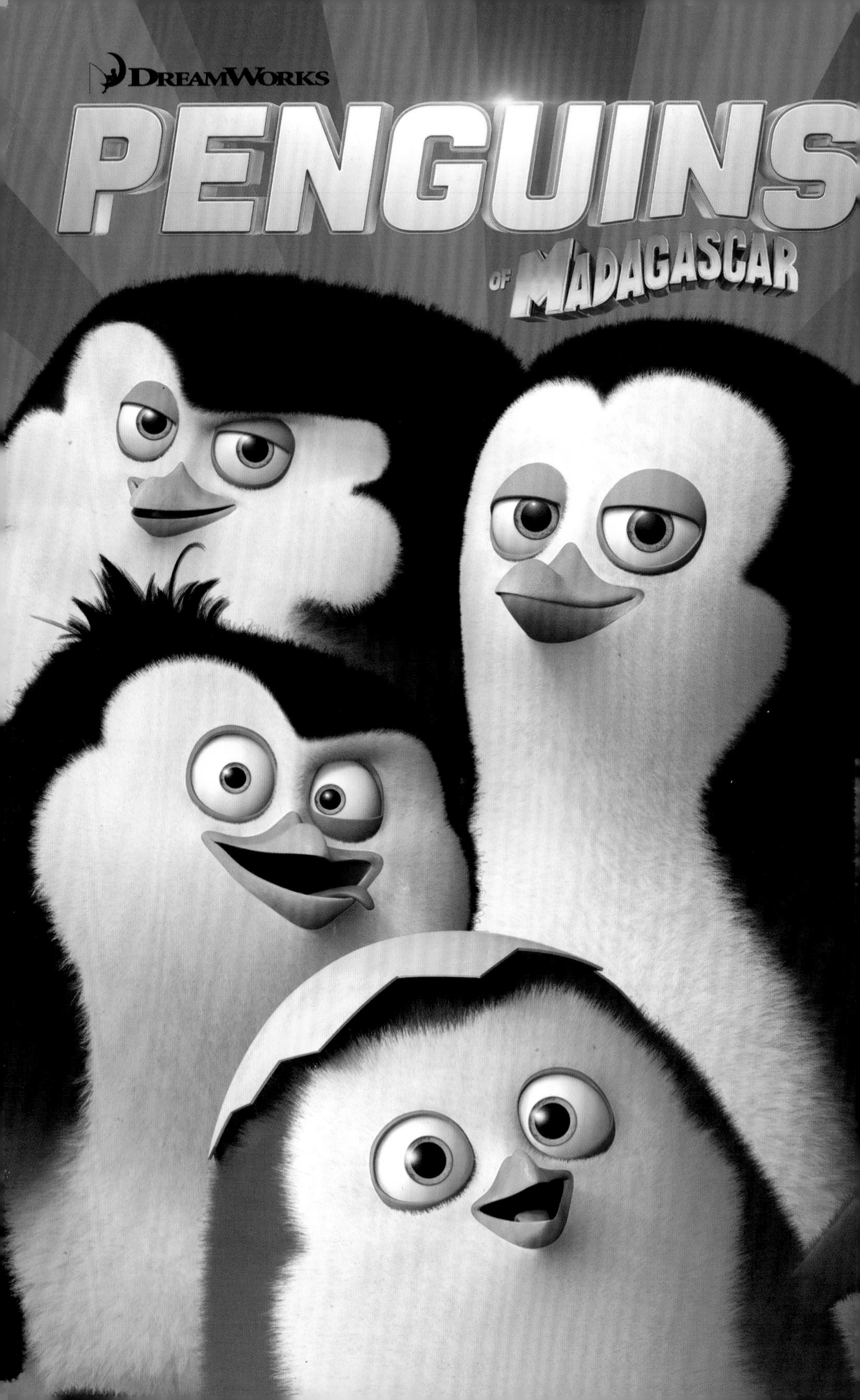
DreamWorks
PENGUINS
OF MADAGASCAR

WHEN IN ROME

SCRIPT
Alex Matthews

PENCILS
Grant Perkins

INKS
Steve Musgrave, Bambos Georgiou
& Robert Wells

COLORS
John Burns and Tanya Roberts

LETTERING
Jim Campbell

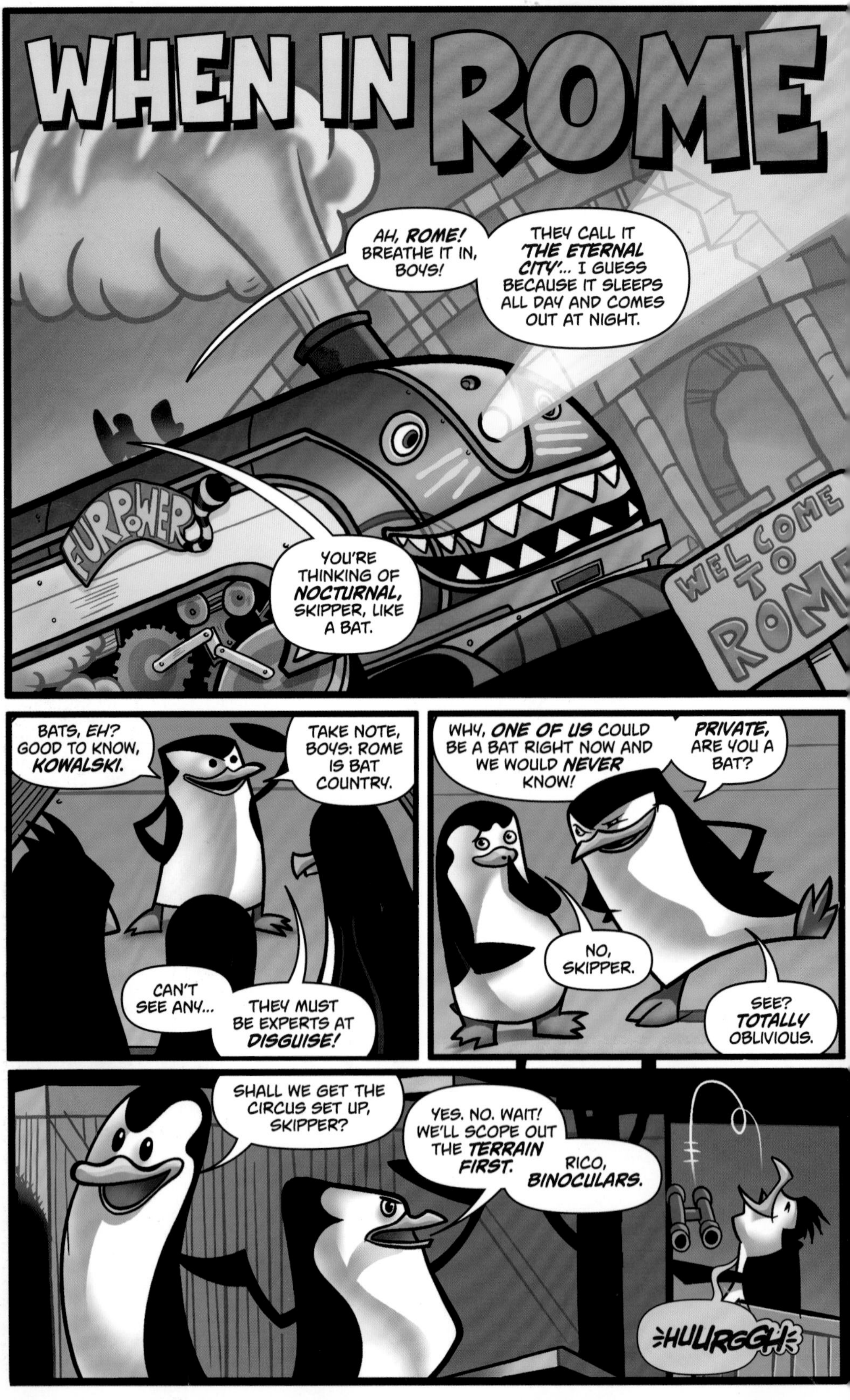
WHEN IN ROME
AH, ROME! BREATHE IT IN, BOYS!
THEY CALL IT 'THE ETERNAL CITY'... I GUESS BECAUSE IT SLEEPS ALL DAY AND COMES OUT AT NIGHT.
FURPOWER
YOU'RE THINKING OF NOCTURNAL, SKIPPER, LIKE A BAT.
WELCOME TO ROME
BATS, EH? GOOD TO KNOW, KOWALSKI.
TAKE NOTE, BOYS: ROME IS BAT COUNTRY.
CAN'T SEE ANY...
THEY MUST BE EXPERTS AT DISGUISE!
WHY, ONE OF US COULD BE A BAT RIGHT NOW AND WE WOULD NEVER KNOW!
PRIVATE, ARE YOU A BAT?
NO, SKIPPER.
SEE? TOTALLY OBLIVIOUS.
SHALL WE GET THE CIRCUS SET UP, SKIPPER?
YES. NO. WAIT! WE'LL SCOPE OUT THE TERRAIN FIRST.
RICO, BINOCULARS.
HUURGGH

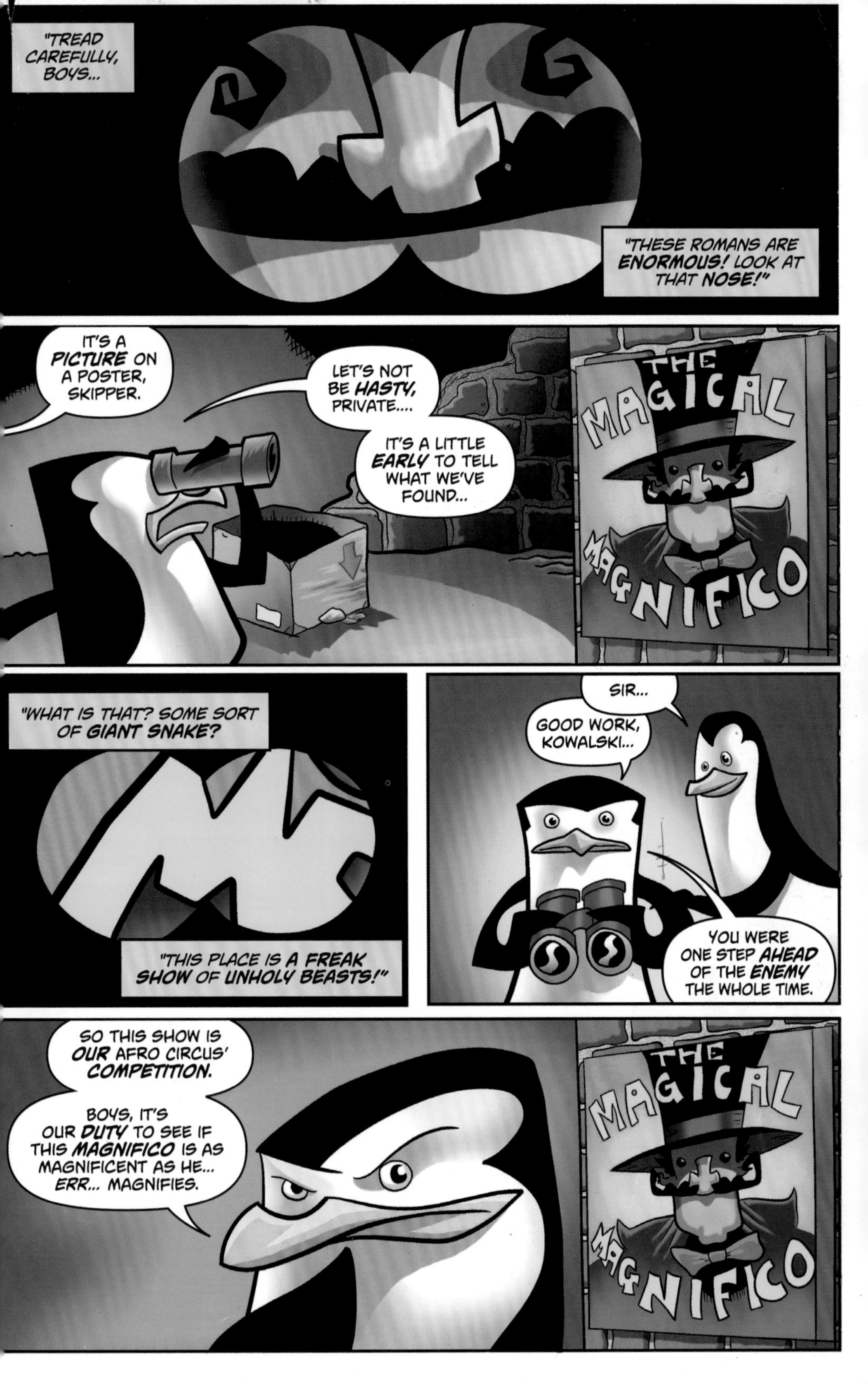
"TREAD CAREFULLY, BOYS...
"THESE ROMANS ARE ENORMOUS! LOOK AT THAT NOSE!"
IT'S A PICTURE ON A POSTER, SKIPPER.
LET'S NOT BE HASTY, PRIVATE....
IT'S A LITTLE EARLY TO TELL WHAT WE'VE FOUND...
THE MAGICAL MAGNIFICO
"WHAT IS THAT? SOME SORT OF GIANT SNAKE?
"THIS PLACE IS A FREAK SHOW OF UNHOLY BEASTS!"
SIR...
GOOD WORK, KOWALSKI...
YOU WERE ONE STEP AHEAD OF THE ENEMY THE WHOLE TIME.
SO THIS SHOW IS OUR AFRO CIRCUS' COMPETITION.
BOYS, IT'S OUR DUTY TO SEE IF THIS MAGNIFICO IS AS MAGNIFICENT AS HE... ERR... MAGNIFIES.
THE MAGICAL MAGNIFICO

SUGGESTIONS?

A FRONTAL ASSAULT WITH A BATTERING RAM ATTACHED TO A TANK, SKIPPER.

OR WE COULD BUY TICKETS.

BOTH GOOD SUGGESTIONS, BUT WE MUST REMEMBER THAT WE'RE HERE ON AN INTELLIGENCE GATHERING MISSION.

PREPARE THE TANK!

FOUR, PLEASE.

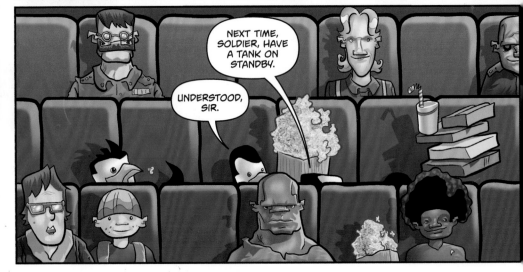

NEXT TIME, SOLDIER, HAVE A TANK ON STANDBY.

UNDERSTOOD, SIR.

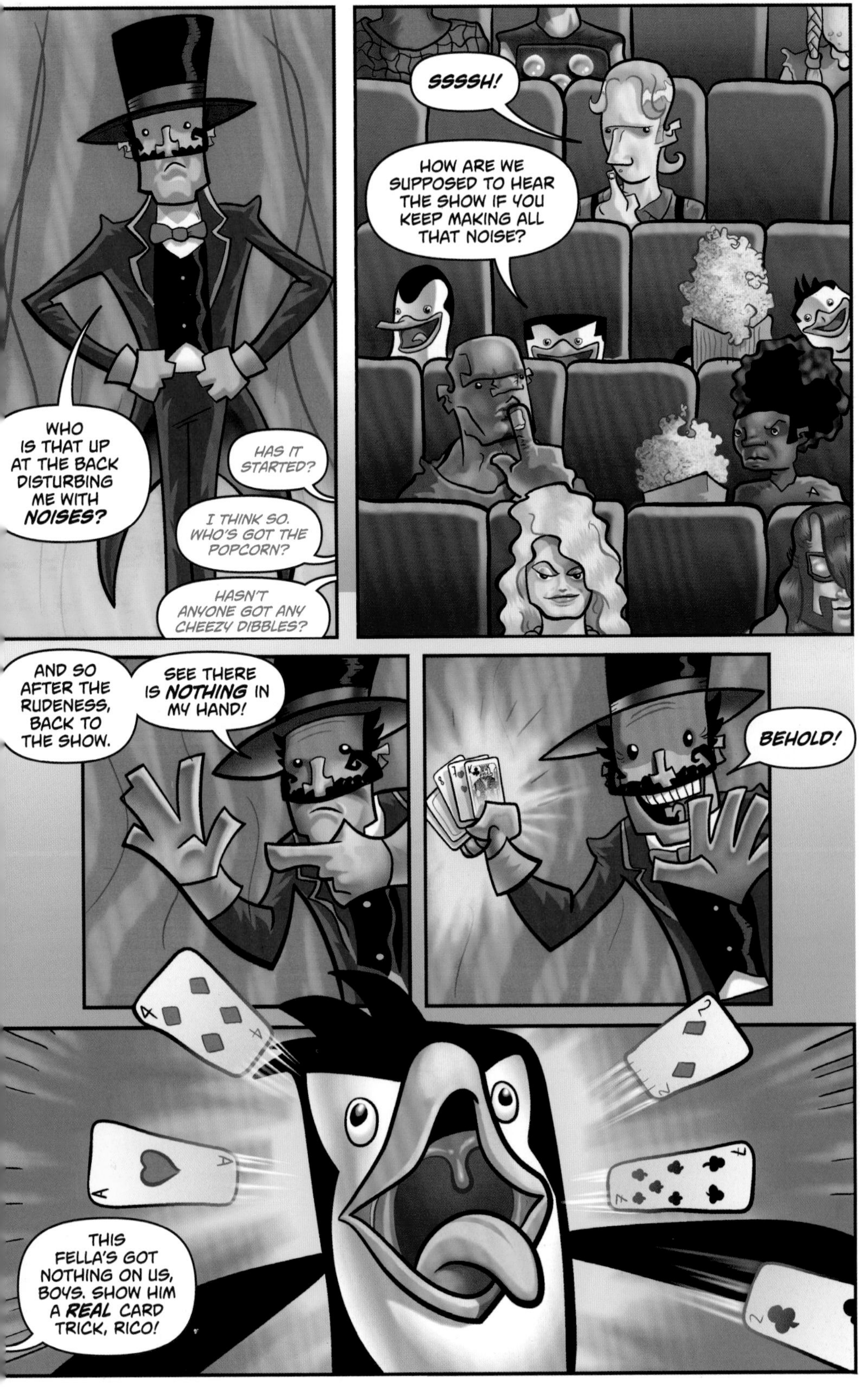
WHO IS THAT UP AT THE BACK DISTURBING ME WITH NOISES?
HAS IT STARTED?
I THINK SO. WHO'S GOT THE POPCORN?
HASN'T ANYONE GOT ANY CHEEZY DIBBLES?
SSSSH!
HOW ARE WE SUPPOSED TO HEAR THE SHOW IF YOU KEEP MAKING ALL THAT NOISE?
AND SO AFTER THE RUDENESS, BACK TO THE SHOW.
SEE THERE IS NOTHING IN MY HAND!
BEHOLD!
THIS FELLA'S GOT NOTHING ON US, BOYS. SHOW HIM A REAL CARD TRICK, RICO!

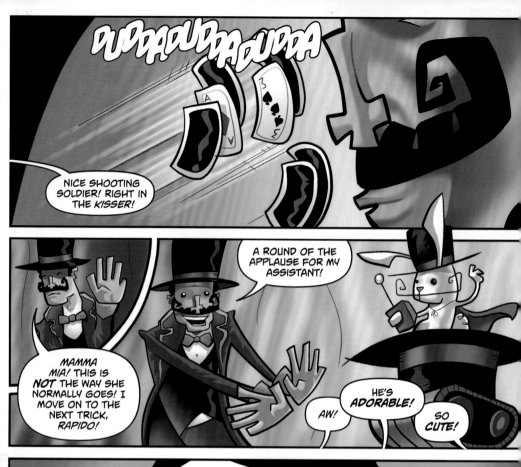

DUDDADUDDADUDDA

NICE SHOOTING SOLDIER! RIGHT IN THE *KISSER!*

A ROUND OF THE APPLAUSE FOR MY ASSISTANT!

MAMMA MIA! THIS IS *NOT* THE WAY SHE NORMALLY GOES! I MOVE ON TO THE NEXT TRICK, *RAPIDO!*

AW!

HE'S *ADORABLE!*

SO *CUTE!*

A *BAT!*

IT'S A *RABBIT*, SKIPPER.

APPEARANCES CAN BE *DECEPTIVE*, KOWALSKI. REMEMBER THE TALE OF THE *DOLPHIN* IN *CAMEL'S CLOTHING?*

I MUST HAVE MISSED THAT ONE.

REMIND ME HOW YOU GOT INTO THIS UNIT, SOLDIER.

SI, HE IS CUTE, BUT HE IS ALSO THE *MISCHIEF MAKER!* WHERE WILL HE APPEAR NEXT?

CLAP CLAP CLAP

LEAVE MY AUDIENCE ALONE, NAUGHTY RABBIT!

AY AY AY! I AM VERY TICKLISH!

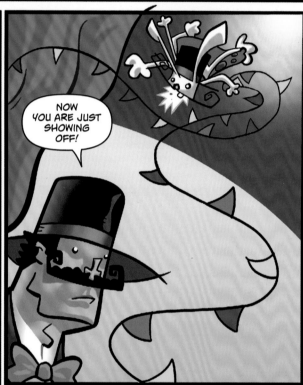

NOW YOU ARE JUST SHOWING OFF!

IT'S NOT NATURAL! IT'S... IT'S *UNAMERICAN!*

EVALUATION, KOWALSKI. HOW IS HE DOING IT?

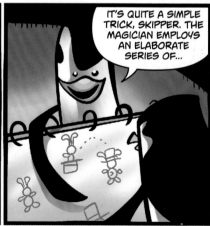

IT'S QUITE A SIMPLE TRICK, SKIPPER. THE MAGICIAN EMPLOYS AN ELABORATE SERIES OF...

PRIVATE, I'M GOING TO NEED YOUR EYES ON THE SHOW WHILE I LISTEN INTENTLY TO EVERY WORD KOWALSKI SAYS.

YOU GOT IT, MR PENGUIN!

CODE RED! WE'VE BEEN *INFILTRATED!*

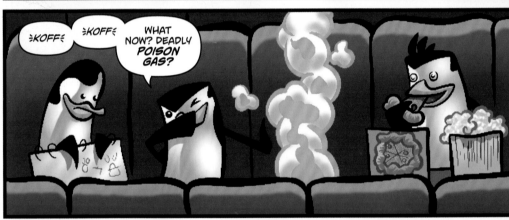

≷KOFF≷ ≷KOFF≷

WHAT NOW? DEADLY *POISON GAS?*

WHAT'S THAT, SKIPPER?

YOU'VE GOT TO HAND IT TO HIM, KOWALSKI, HE KNOWS A THING OR TWO ABOUT THE MAGICAL ARTS!

GRAZIE! THAT'S A VERY NICE THING TO SAY!

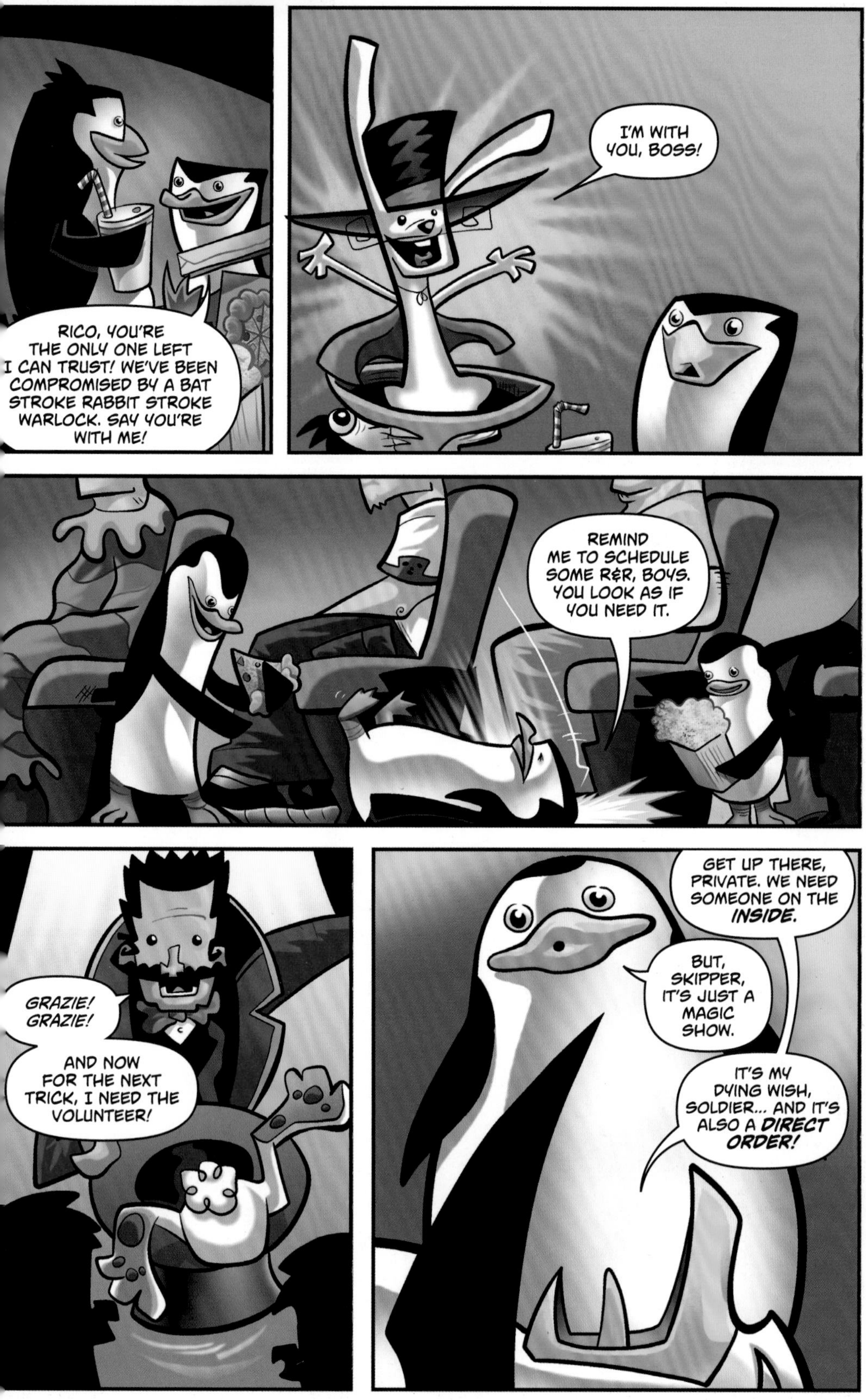
RICO, YOU'RE THE ONLY ONE LEFT I CAN TRUST! WE'VE BEEN COMPROMISED BY A BAT STROKE RABBIT STROKE WARLOCK. SAY YOU'RE WITH ME!
I'M WITH YOU, BOSS!
REMIND ME TO SCHEDULE SOME R&R, BOYS. YOU LOOK AS IF YOU NEED IT.
GRAZIE! GRAZIE!
AND NOW FOR THE NEXT TRICK, I NEED THE VOLUNTEER!
GET UP THERE, PRIVATE. WE NEED SOMEONE ON THE *INSIDE*.
BUT, SKIPPER, IT'S JUST A MAGIC SHOW.
IT'S MY DYING WISH, SOLDIER... AND IT'S ALSO A ***DIRECT ORDER!***

WELCOME TO THE STAGE, THE BRAVE VOLUNTEER... UM... PENGUIN!

HELLO!

THE SAWING OF THE PENGUIN IN HALF IS THE CLASSIC TRICK, BUT MAGNIFICO HAS PUT HIS OWN MAGNIFICO TWIST ON IT!

SKIPPER, LOOK, I'M IN SHOW BUSINESS!

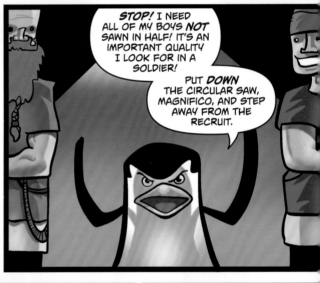

STOP! I NEED ALL OF MY BOYS NOT SAWN IN HALF! IT'S AN IMPORTANT QUALITY I LOOK FOR IN A SOLDIER!

PUT DOWN THE CIRCULAR SAW, MAGNIFICO, AND STEP AWAY FROM THE RECRUIT.

SKIPPER, IT'S ALL JUST AN ILLUSION. TO MAKE IT LOOK REAL THE MAGICIAN HAS SET UP A...

THE TIME FOR TALK IS OVER, KOWALSKI. NOW IT'S TIME FOR...

SECURITY!

SHOUTING! SEE, THIS GUY GETS IT.

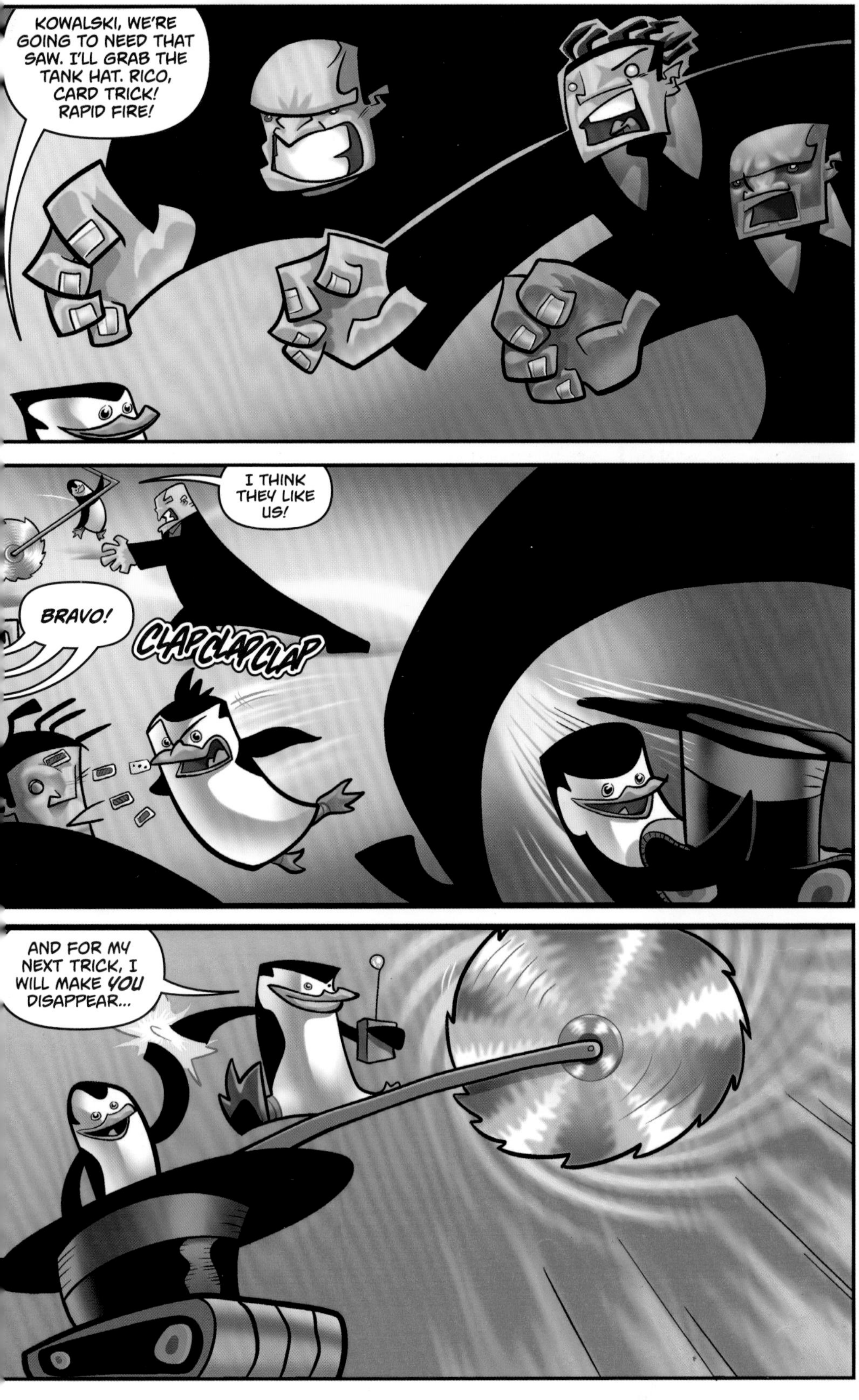
KOWALSKI, WE'RE GOING TO NEED THAT SAW. I'LL GRAB THE TANK HAT. RICO, CARD TRICK! RAPID FIRE!
I THINK THEY LIKE US!
BRAVO!
CLAP CLAP CLAP
AND FOR MY NEXT TRICK, I WILL MAKE YOU DISAPPEAR...

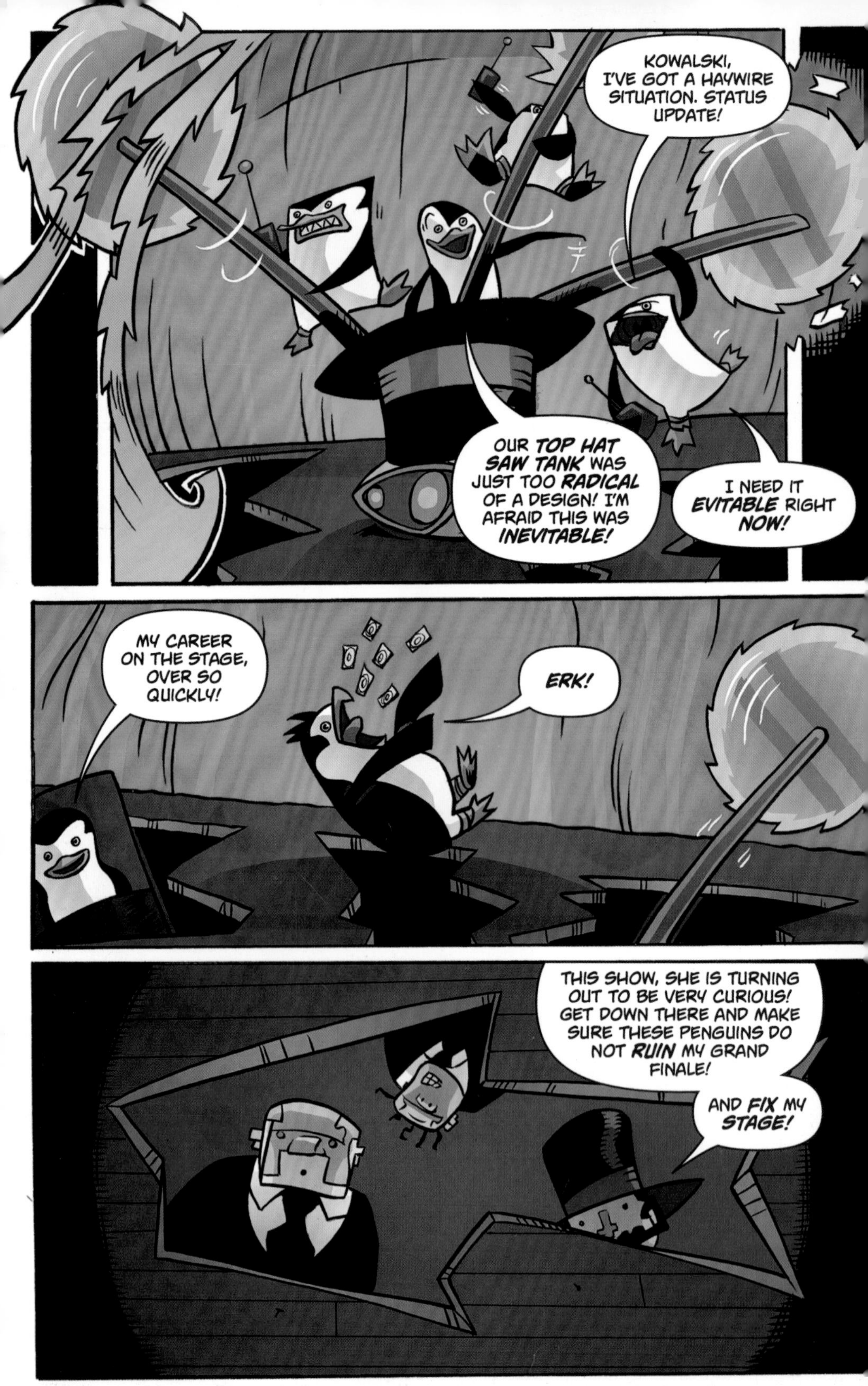
KOWALSKI, I'VE GOT A HAYWIRE SITUATION. STATUS UPDATE!
OUR TOP HAT SAW TANK WAS JUST TOO RADICAL OF A DESIGN! I'M AFRAID THIS WAS INEVITABLE!
I NEED IT EVITABLE RIGHT NOW!
MY CAREER ON THE STAGE, OVER SO QUICKLY!
ERK!
THIS SHOW, SHE IS TURNING OUT TO BE VERY CURIOUS! GET DOWN THERE AND MAKE SURE THESE PENGUINS DO NOT RUIN MY GRAND FINALE!
AND FIX MY STAGE!

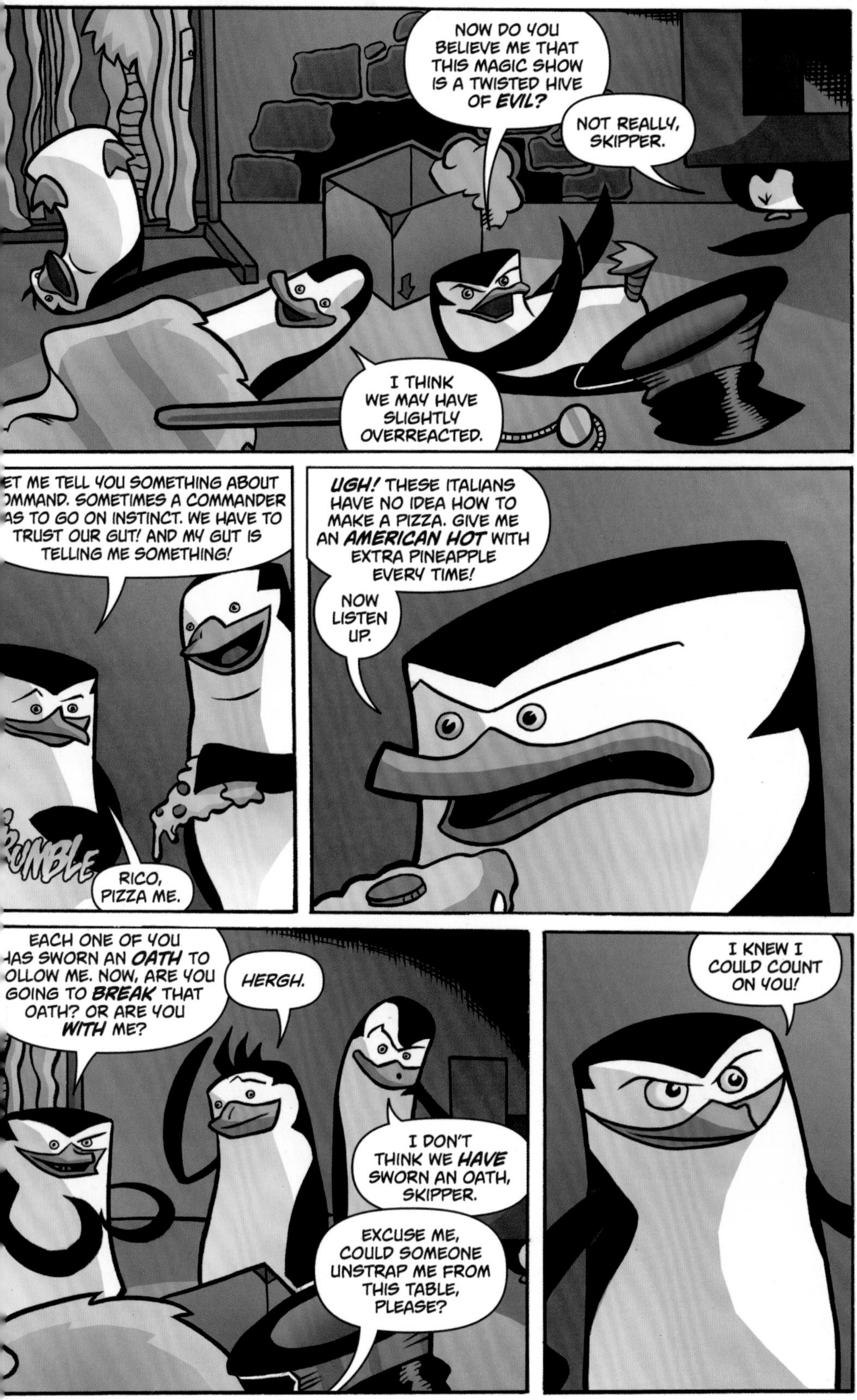
NOW DO YOU BELIEVE ME THAT THIS MAGIC SHOW IS A TWISTED HIVE OF EVIL?
NOT REALLY, SKIPPER.
I THINK WE MAY HAVE SLIGHTLY OVERREACTED.
ET ME TELL YOU SOMETHING ABOUT OMMAND. SOMETIMES A COMMANDER AS TO GO ON INSTINCT. WE HAVE TO TRUST OUR GUT! AND MY GUT IS TELLING ME SOMETHING!
RUMBLE
RICO, PIZZA ME.
UGH! THESE ITALIANS HAVE NO IDEA HOW TO MAKE A PIZZA. GIVE ME AN AMERICAN HOT WITH EXTRA PINEAPPLE EVERY TIME!
NOW LISTEN UP.
EACH ONE OF YOU HAS SWORN AN OATH TO OLLOW ME. NOW, ARE YOU GOING TO BREAK THAT OATH? OR ARE YOU WITH ME?
HERGH.
I DON'T THINK WE HAVE SWORN AN OATH, SKIPPER.
EXCUSE ME, COULD SOMEONE UNSTRAP ME FROM THIS TABLE, PLEASE?
I KNEW I COULD COUNT ON YOU!

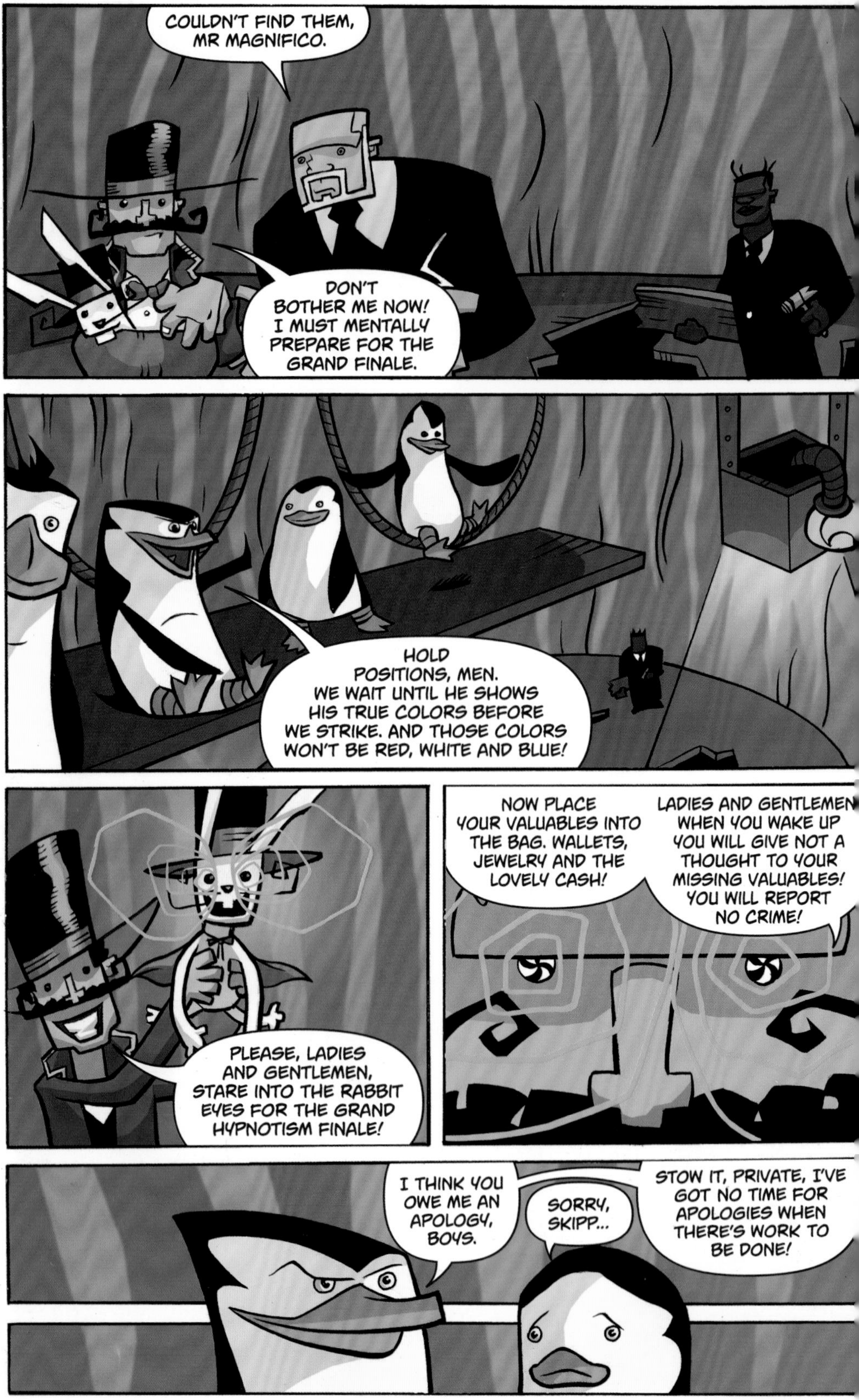
COULDN'T FIND THEM, MR MAGNIFICO.
DON'T BOTHER ME NOW! I MUST MENTALLY PREPARE FOR THE GRAND FINALE.
HOLD POSITIONS, MEN. WE WAIT UNTIL HE SHOWS HIS TRUE COLORS BEFORE WE STRIKE. AND THOSE COLORS WON'T BE RED, WHITE AND BLUE!
PLEASE, LADIES AND GENTLEMEN, STARE INTO THE RABBIT EYES FOR THE GRAND HYPNOTISM FINALE!
NOW PLACE YOUR VALUABLES INTO THE BAG. WALLETS, JEWELRY AND THE LOVELY CASH!
LADIES AND GENTLEMEN WHEN YOU WAKE UP YOU WILL GIVE NOT A THOUGHT TO YOUR MISSING VALUABLES! YOU WILL REPORT NO CRIME!
I THINK YOU OWE ME AN APOLOGY, BOYS.
SORRY, SKIPP...
STOW IT, PRIVATE, I'VE GOT NO TIME FOR APOLOGIES WHEN THERE'S WORK TO BE DONE!

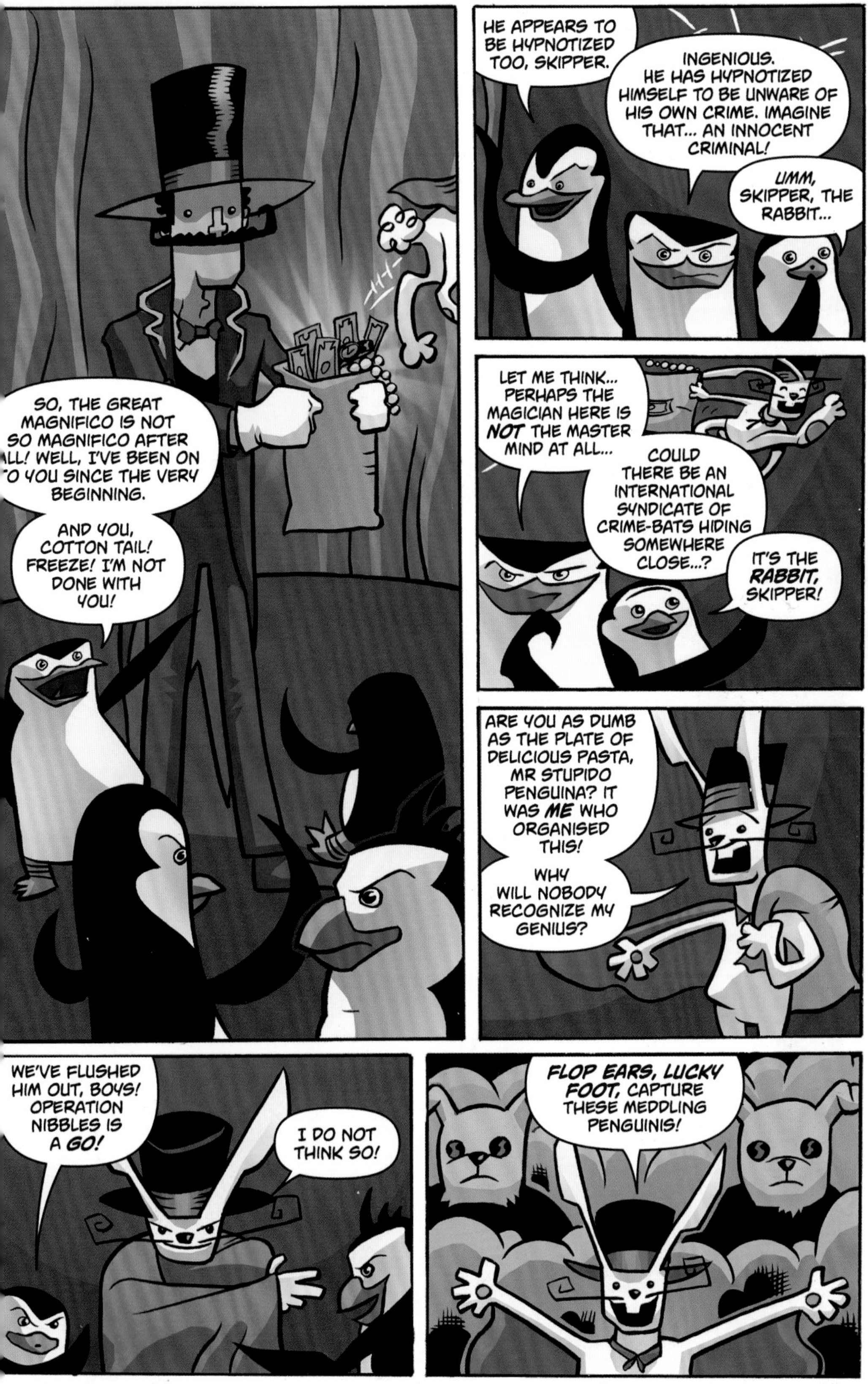

SO, THE GREAT MAGNIFICO IS NOT SO MAGNIFICO AFTER ALL! WELL, I'VE BEEN ON TO YOU SINCE THE VERY BEGINNING.
AND YOU, COTTON TAIL! FREEZE! I'M NOT DONE WITH YOU!
HE APPEARS TO BE HYPNOTIZED TOO, SKIPPER.
INGENIOUS. HE HAS HYPNOTIZED HIMSELF TO BE UNWARE OF HIS OWN CRIME. IMAGINE THAT... AN INNOCENT CRIMINAL!
UMM, SKIPPER, THE RABBIT...
LET ME THINK... PERHAPS THE MAGICIAN HERE IS NOT THE MASTER MIND AT ALL...
COULD THERE BE AN INTERNATIONAL SYNDICATE OF CRIME-BATS HIDING SOMEWHERE CLOSE...?
IT'S THE RABBIT, SKIPPER!
ARE YOU AS DUMB AS THE PLATE OF DELICIOUS PASTA, MR STUPIDO PENGUINA? IT WAS ME WHO ORGANISED THIS!
WHY WILL NOBODY RECOGNIZE MY GENIUS?
WE'VE FLUSHED HIM OUT, BOYS! OPERATION NIBBLES IS A GO!
I DO NOT THINK SO!
FLOP EARS, LUCKY FOOT, CAPTURE THESE MEDDLING PENGUINIS!

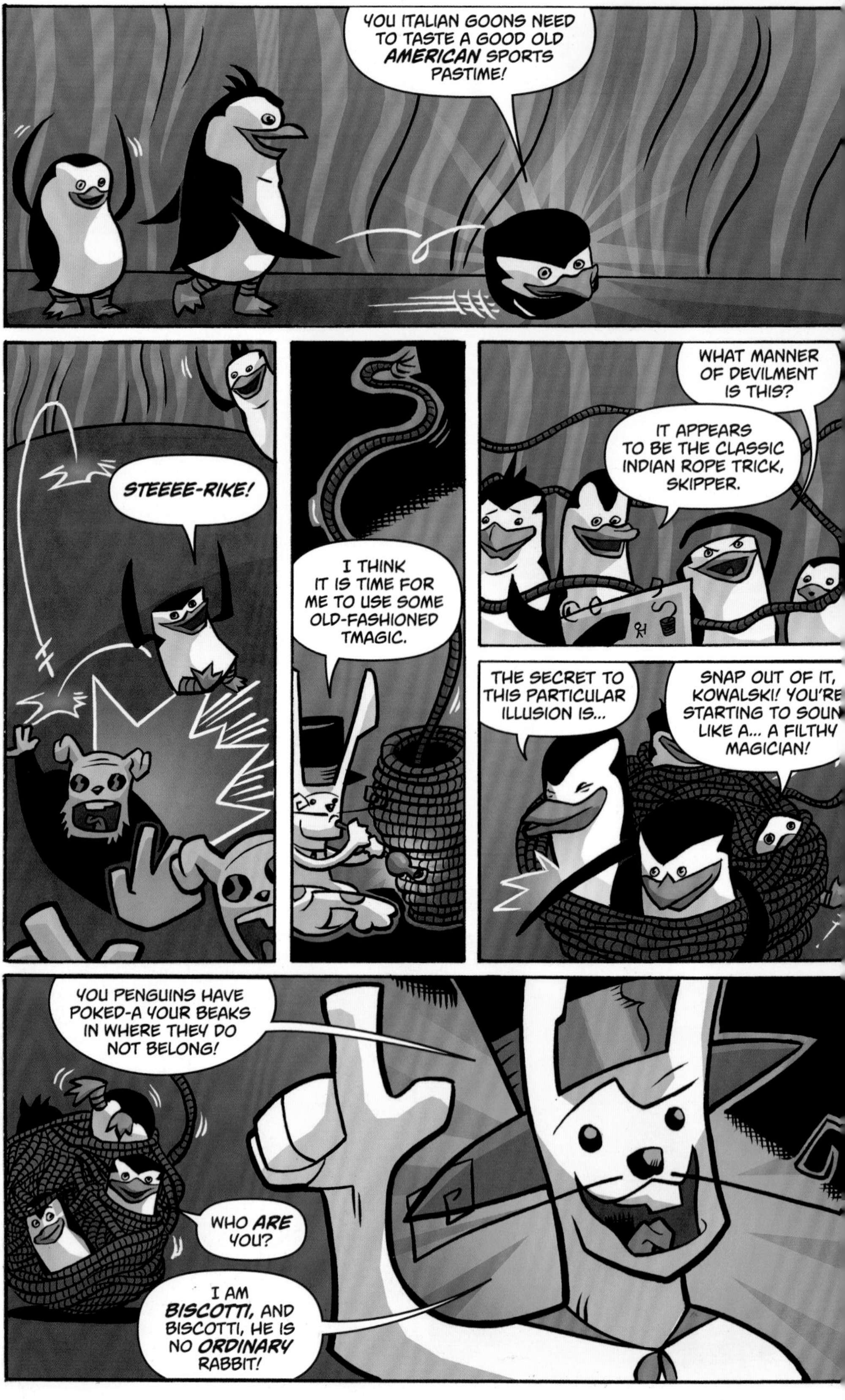
YOU ITALIAN GOONS NEED TO TASTE A GOOD OLD AMERICAN SPORTS PASTIME!
STEEEE-RIKE!
I THINK IT IS TIME FOR ME TO USE SOME OLD-FASHIONED TMAGIC.
WHAT MANNER OF DEVILMENT IS THIS?
IT APPEARS TO BE THE CLASSIC INDIAN ROPE TRICK, SKIPPER.
THE SECRET TO THIS PARTICULAR ILLUSION IS...
SNAP OUT OF IT, KOWALSKI! YOU'RE STARTING TO SOUN LIKE A... A FILTHY MAGICIAN!
YOU PENGUINS HAVE POKED-A YOUR BEAKS IN WHERE THEY DO NOT BELONG!
WHO ARE YOU?
I AM BISCOTTI, AND BISCOTTI, HE IS NO ORDINARY RABBIT!

BISCOTTI? TRANSLATION, KOWALSKI.

IT MEANS BISCUIT, SKIPPER.

BISCUIT? HOW *ADORABLE*. BOYS, CUTENESS APPRECIATION MODE!

AWWWW! BISCUIT, THE COOT ICKLE BUNNY WABBIT!

SILENCE! YOU WILL TAKE ME SERIOUSLY AS I TELL YOU MY BACK-STORY!

YES, IT IS *I* WHO IS THE GENIUS BEHIND THIS CRIMINAL MAGIC SHOW.

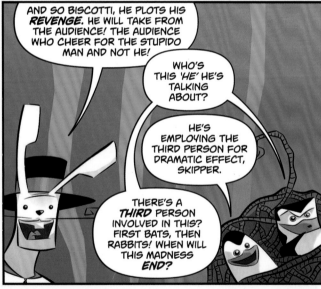

MANY YEARS AGO I TRY TO START MY OWN SHOW BUT NO-ONE WILL TAKE SERIOUSLY THE RABBIT MAGICIAN WITH HIS CUTE TWITCHY NOSE AND LITTLE COTTON TAIL!

AND SO I HAVE TO *TEACH* THIS MAGNIFICO! MORE LIKE THE MAGNIFICO *IDIOT!* DOES HE APPRECIATE BISCOTTI? NO, HE DOES NOT!

AND SO BISCOTTI, HE PLOTS HIS *REVENGE.* HE WILL TAKE FROM THE AUDIENCE! THE AUDIENCE WHO CHEER FOR THE STUPIDO MAN AND NOT HE!

WHO'S THIS '*HE*' HE'S TALKING ABOUT?

HE'S EMPLOYING THE THIRD PERSON FOR DRAMATIC EFFECT, SKIPPER.

THERE'S A *THIRD* PERSON INVOLVED IN THIS? FIRST BATS, THEN RABBITS! WHEN WILL THIS MADNESS *END?*

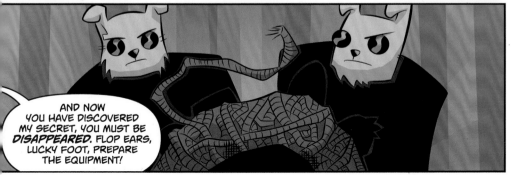

AND NOW YOU HAVE DISCOVERED MY SECRET, YOU MUST BE *DISAPPEARED.* FLOP EARS, LUCKY FOOT, PREPARE THE EQUIPMENT!

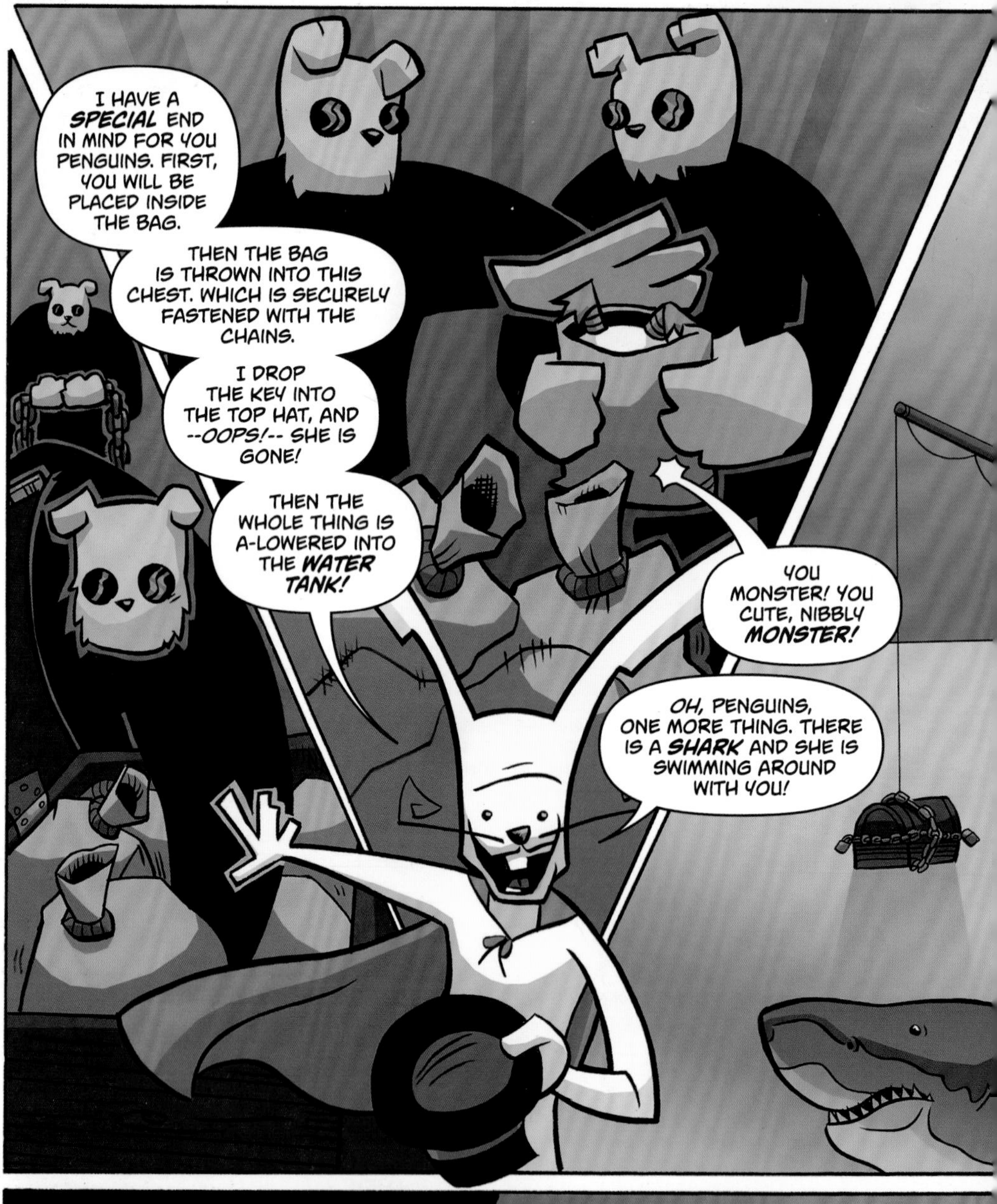
I HAVE A SPECIAL END IN MIND FOR YOU PENGUINS. FIRST, YOU WILL BE PLACED INSIDE THE BAG.
THEN THE BAG IS THROWN INTO THIS CHEST. WHICH IS SECURELY FASTENED WITH THE CHAINS.
I DROP THE KEY INTO THE TOP HAT, AND --OOPS!-- SHE IS GONE!
THEN THE WHOLE THING IS A-LOWERED INTO THE WATER TANK!
YOU MONSTER! YOU CUTE, NIBBLY MONSTER!
OH, PENGUINS, ONE MORE THING. THERE IS A SHARK AND SHE IS SWIMMING AROUND WITH YOU!
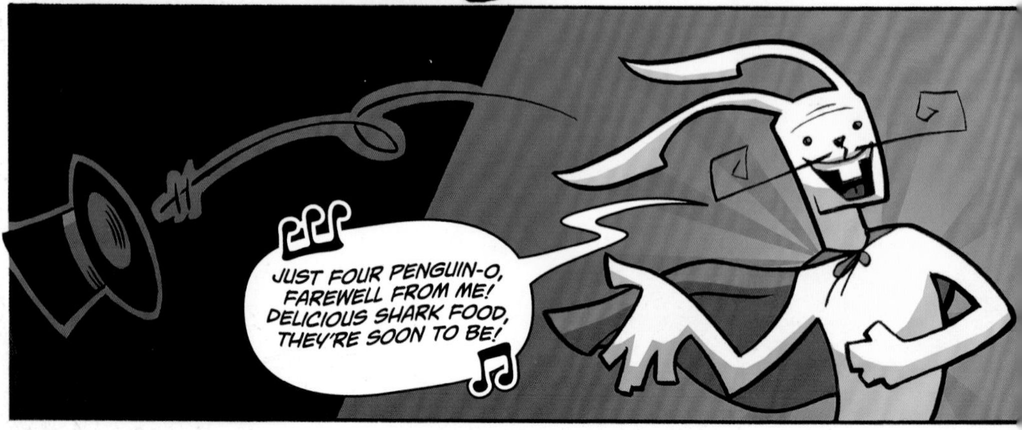
JUST FOUR PENGUIN-O, FAREWELL FROM ME! DELICIOUS SHARK FOOD, THEY'RE SOON TO BE!

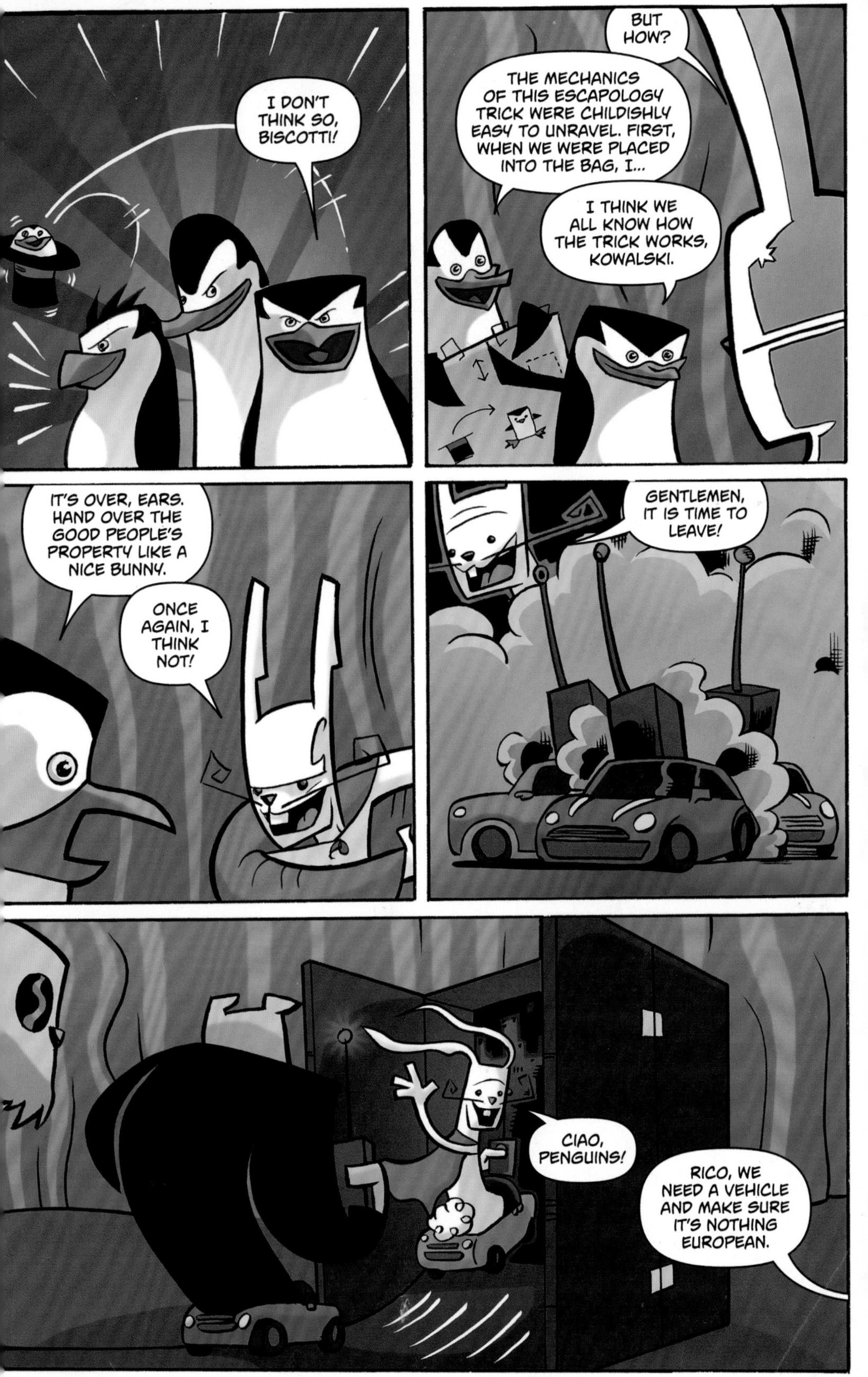
I DON'T THINK SO, BISCOTTI!
BUT HOW?
THE MECHANICS OF THIS ESCAPOLOGY TRICK WERE CHILDISHLY EASY TO UNRAVEL. FIRST, WHEN WE WERE PLACED INTO THE BAG, I...
I THINK WE ALL KNOW HOW THE TRICK WORKS, KOWALSKI.
IT'S OVER, EARS. HAND OVER THE GOOD PEOPLE'S PROPERTY LIKE A NICE BUNNY.
ONCE AGAIN, I THINK NOT!
GENTLEMEN, IT IS TIME TO LEAVE!
CIAO, PENGUINS!
RICO, WE NEED A VEHICLE AND MAKE SURE IT'S NOTHING EUROPEAN.

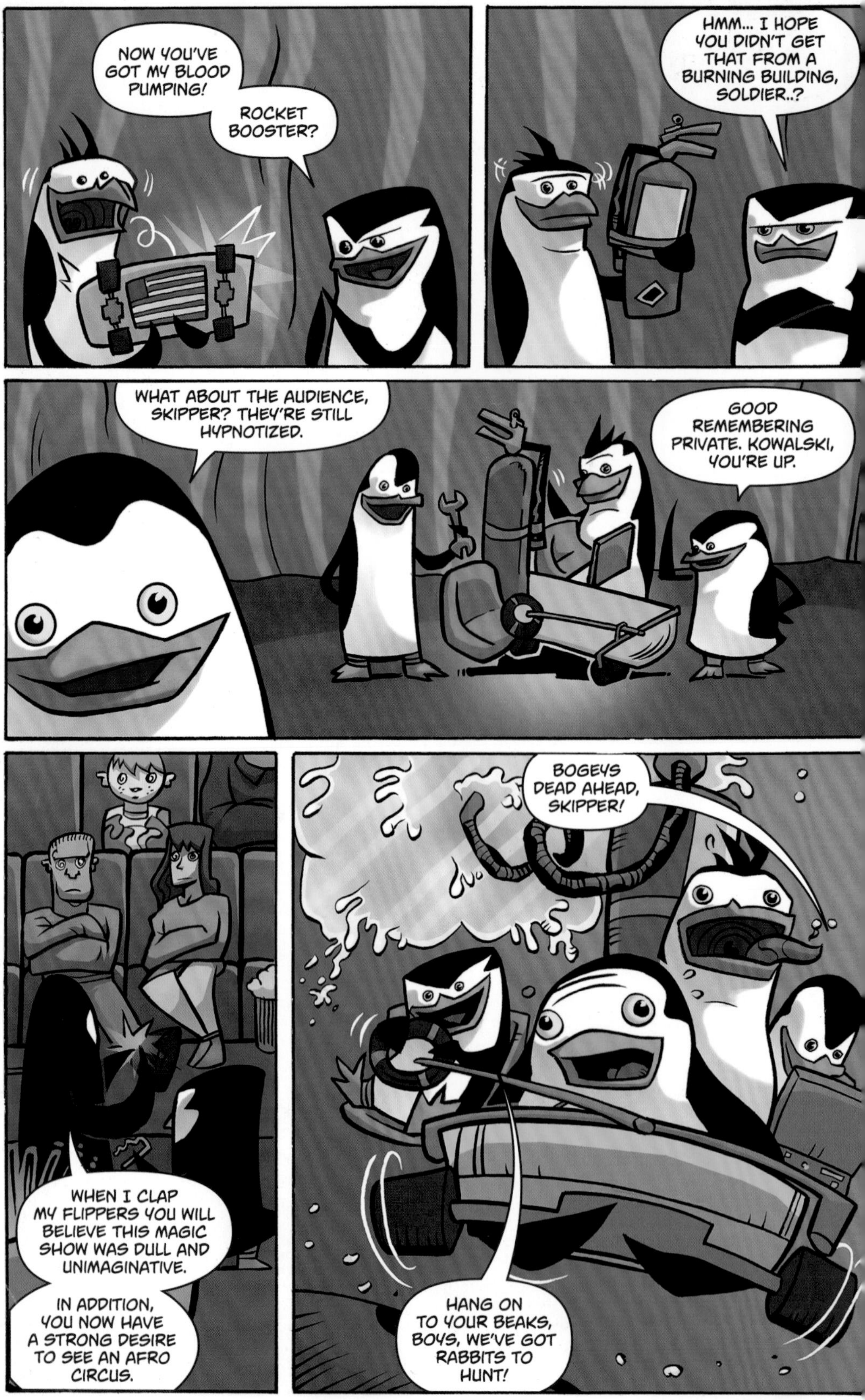
NOW YOU'VE GOT MY BLOOD PUMPING!
ROCKET BOOSTER?
HMM... I HOPE YOU DIDN'T GET THAT FROM A BURNING BUILDING, SOLDIER..?
WHAT ABOUT THE AUDIENCE, SKIPPER? THEY'RE STILL HYPNOTIZED.
GOOD REMEMBERING PRIVATE. KOWALSKI, YOU'RE UP.
WHEN I CLAP MY FLIPPERS YOU WILL BELIEVE THIS MAGIC SHOW WAS DULL AND UNIMAGINATIVE.
IN ADDITION, YOU NOW HAVE A STRONG DESIRE TO SEE AN AFRO CIRCUS.
BOGEYS DEAD AHEAD, SKIPPER!
HANG ON TO YOUR BEAKS, BOYS, WE'VE GOT RABBITS TO HUNT!

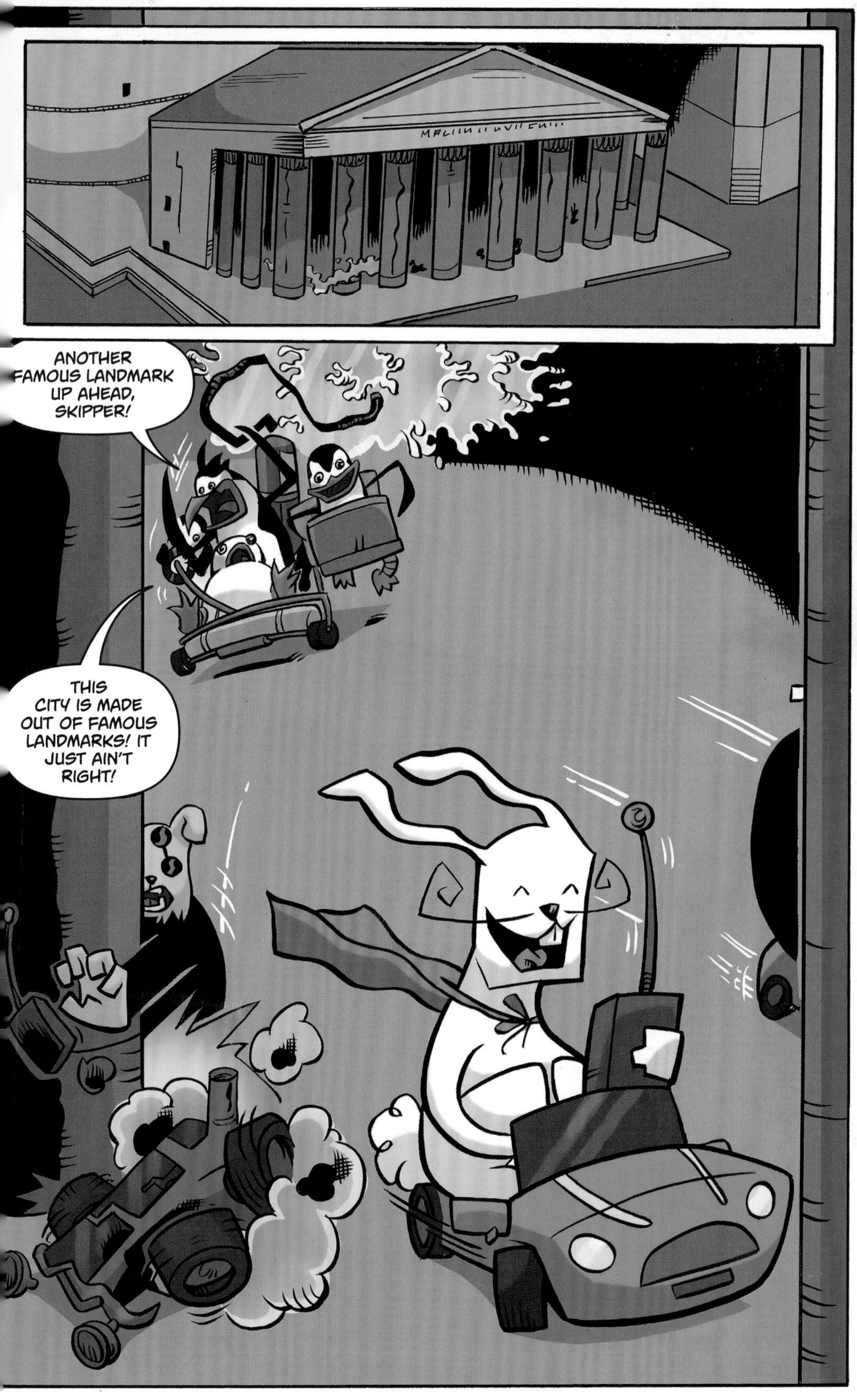
ANOTHER FAMOUS LANDMARK UP AHEAD, SKIPPER!
THIS CITY IS MADE OUT OF FAMOUS LANDMARKS! IT JUST AIN'T RIGHT!

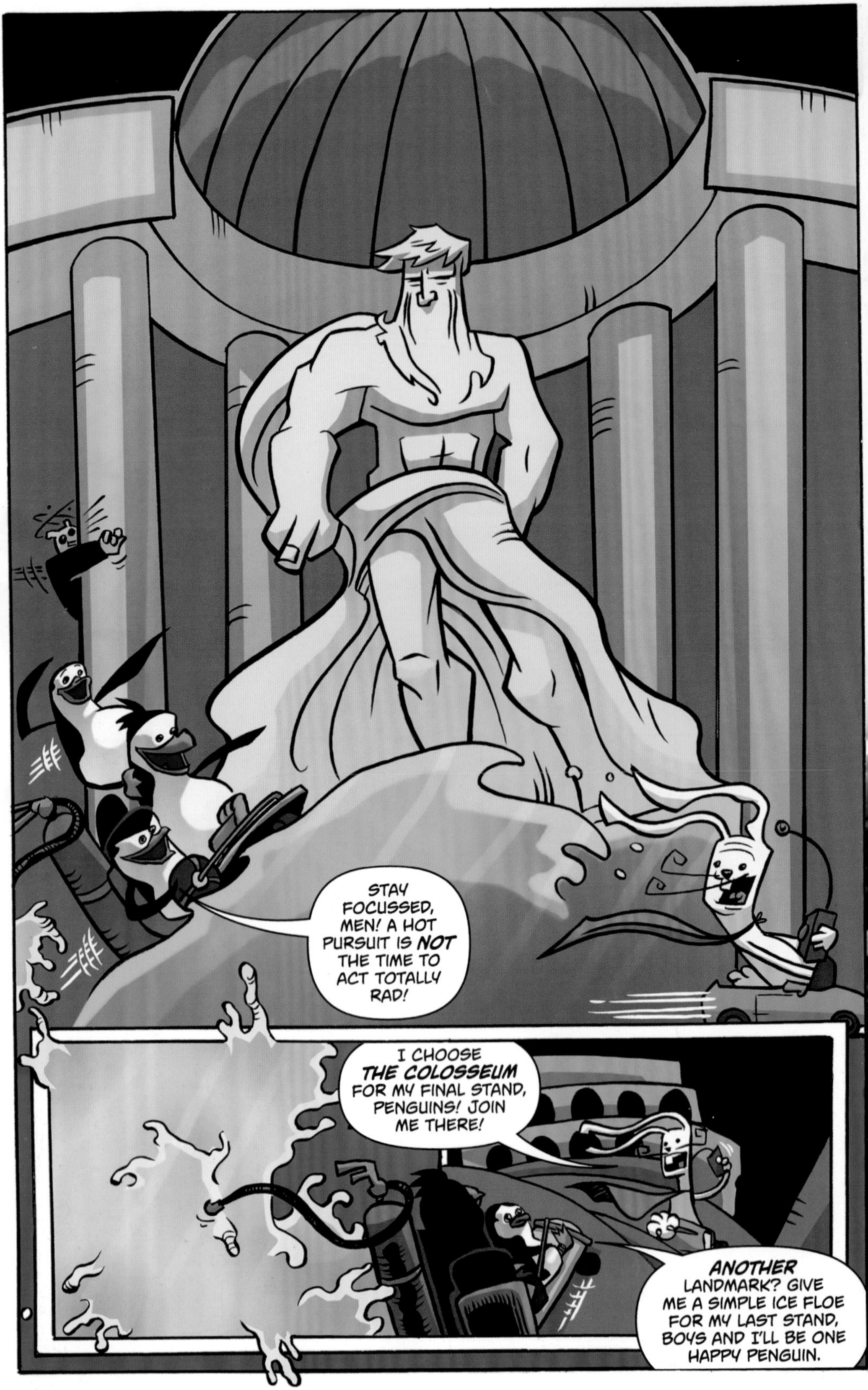
STAY FOCUSSED, MEN! A HOT PURSUIT IS NOT THE TIME TO ACT TOTALLY RAD!
I CHOOSE THE COLOSSEUM FOR MY FINAL STAND, PENGUINS! JOIN ME THERE!
ANOTHER LANDMARK? GIVE ME A SIMPLE ICE FLOE FOR MY LAST STAND, BOYS AND I'LL BE ONE HAPPY PENGUIN.

GIVE IT UP, HOPPITY, YOU'VE GOT NOWHERE TO GO.

YOU THINK YOU HAVE ME CORNERED, PENGUINO? A GREAT MAGICIAN IS *NEVER* CORNERED!

WE'RE *READY* FOR YOUR HYPNOTISM, SCONE.

MY NAME IS *NOT* SCONE!

HYPNOTISM, *PAH!* TOO EASY! HERE, IN THE GREATEST ARENA ON EARTH, I SHALL PULL OFF THE *GREATEST TRICK* EVER PERFORMED, AND YOU PENGUINS SHALL BE MY *AUDIENCE!*

YOU TALK BIG, BISCOTTI, BUT YOU'RE ONE COOKIE THAT ISN'T GOING TO GET THE MILK!

THAT DOESN'T MAKE MUCH SENSE, SKIPPER.

JUSTICE DOESN'T MAKE MUCH SENSE, KOWALSKI!

I THINK IT DOES, SKIPPER.

ARRIVEDERCI, PENGUINS! PERHAPS WE WILL MEET AGAIN.

STOP THAT FLUFFY MANIAC!

HOW DID HE *DO* THAT?

KOWALSKI, I NEED ANSWERS, *PRONTO!*

I... I... I DON'T HAVE A *CLUE*, SKIPPER.

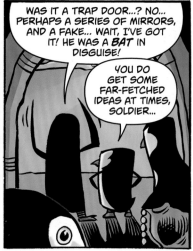

WAS IT A TRAP DOOR...? NO... PERHAPS A SERIES OF MIRRORS, AND A FAKE... WAIT, I'VE GOT IT! HE WAS A *BAT* IN DISGUISE!

YOU DO GET SOME FAR-FETCHED IDEAS AT TIMES, SOLDIER...

THE END!

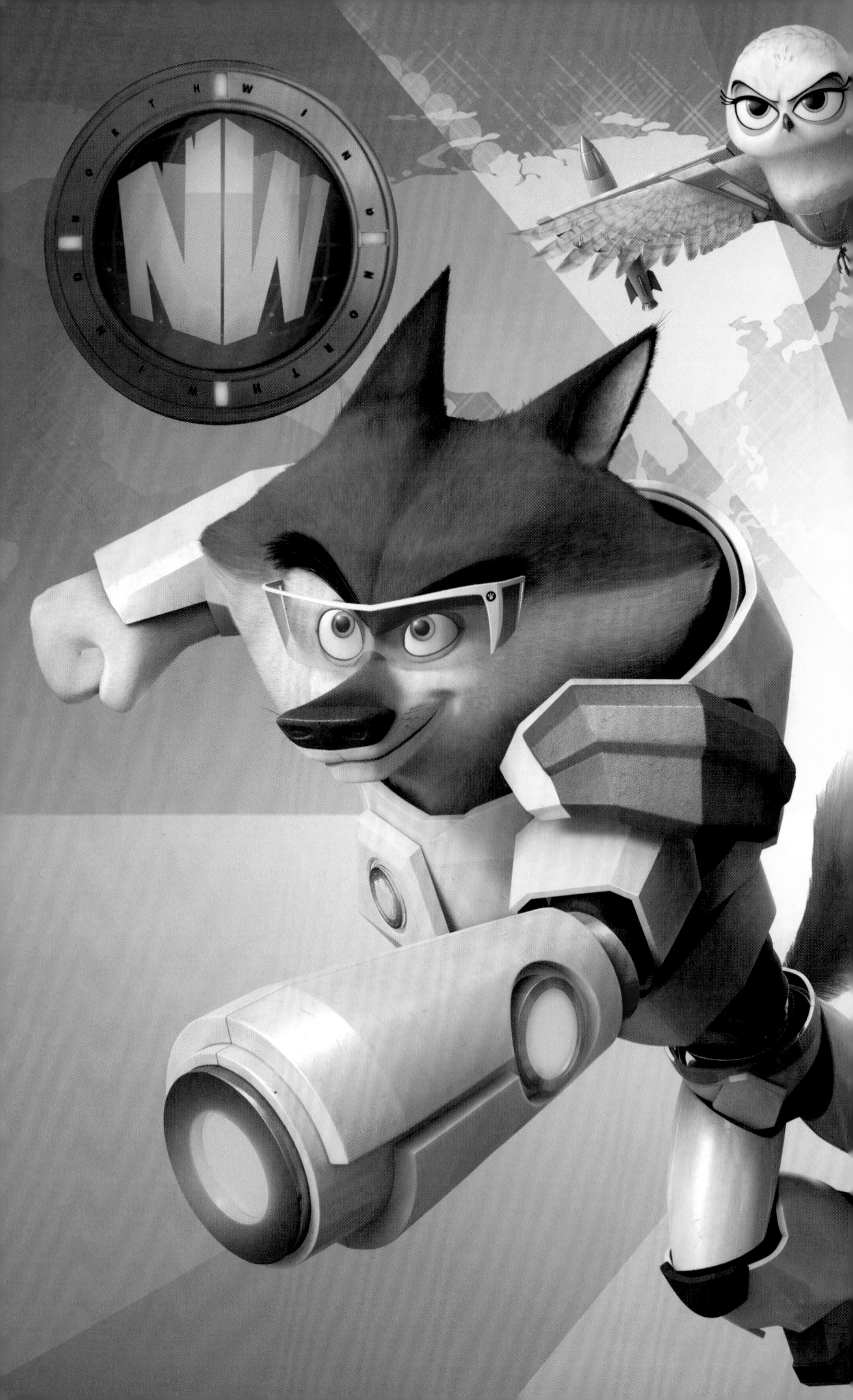
NORTH WIND
NW

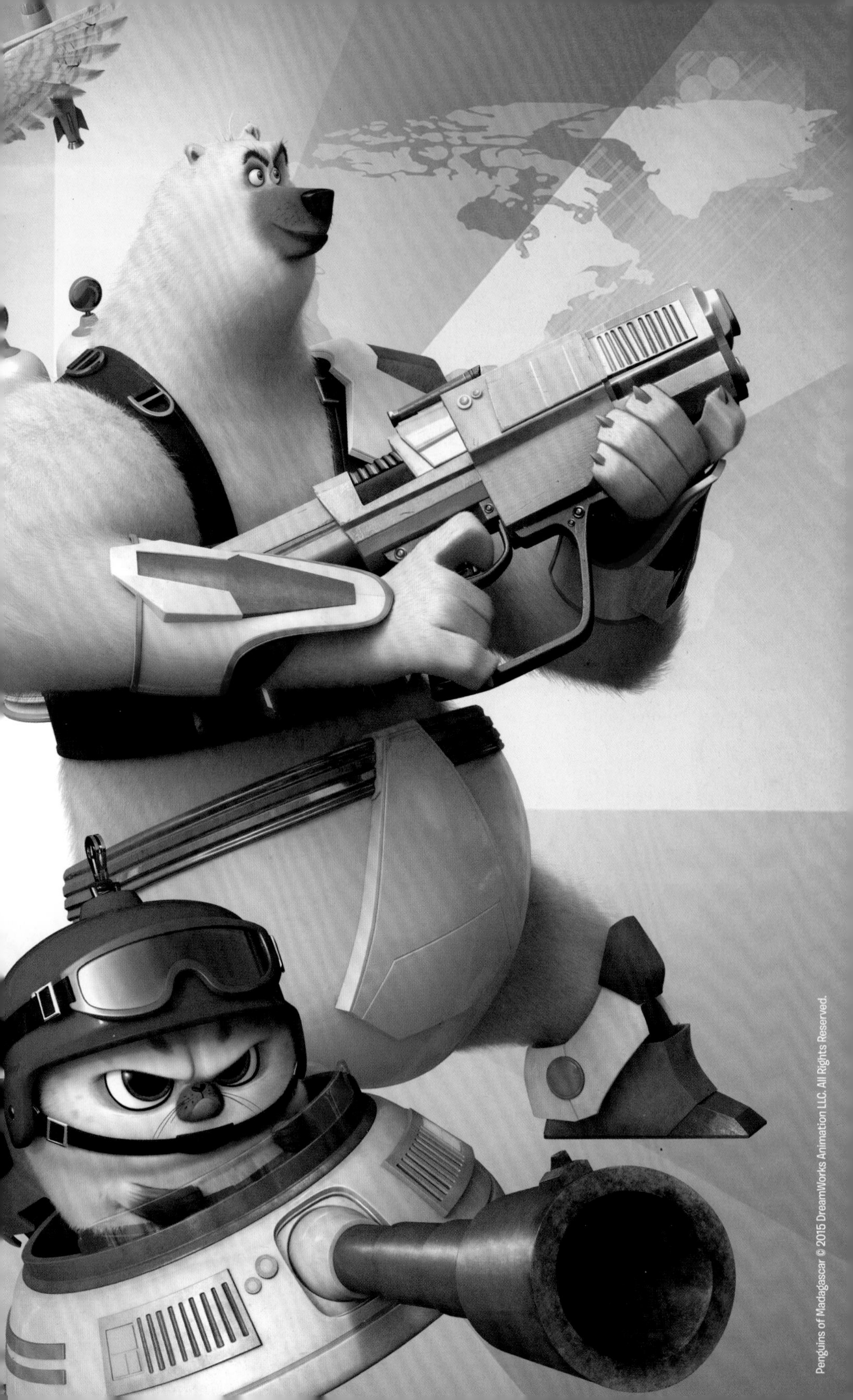

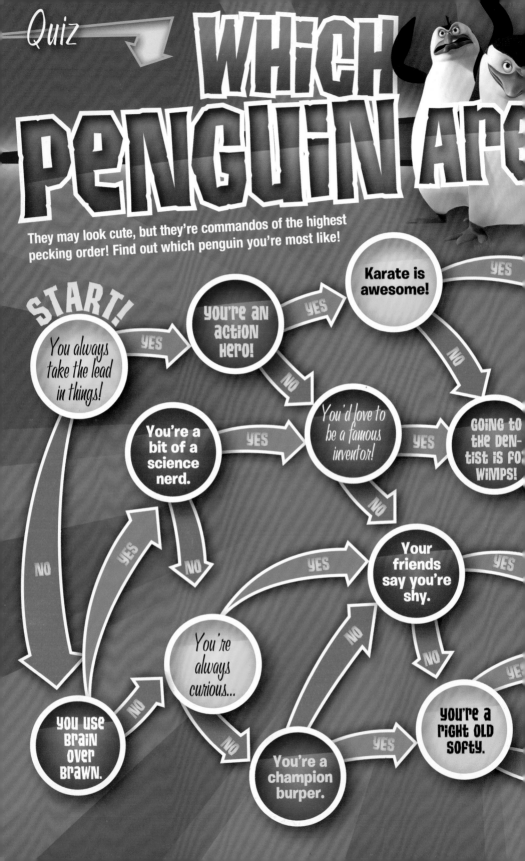

Quiz

WHICH PENGUIN ARE

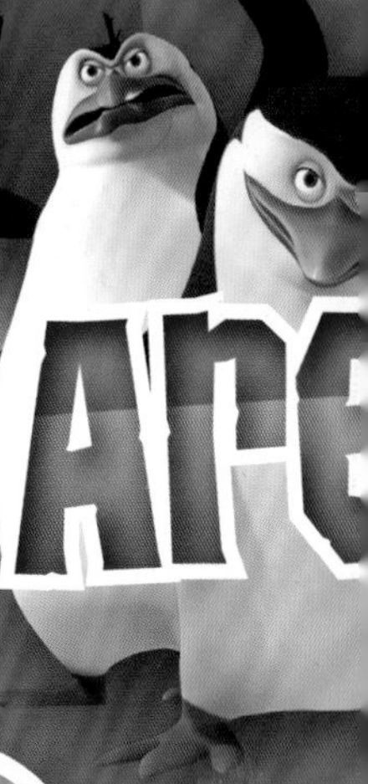

They may look cute, but they're commandos of the highest pecking order! Find out which penguin you're most like!

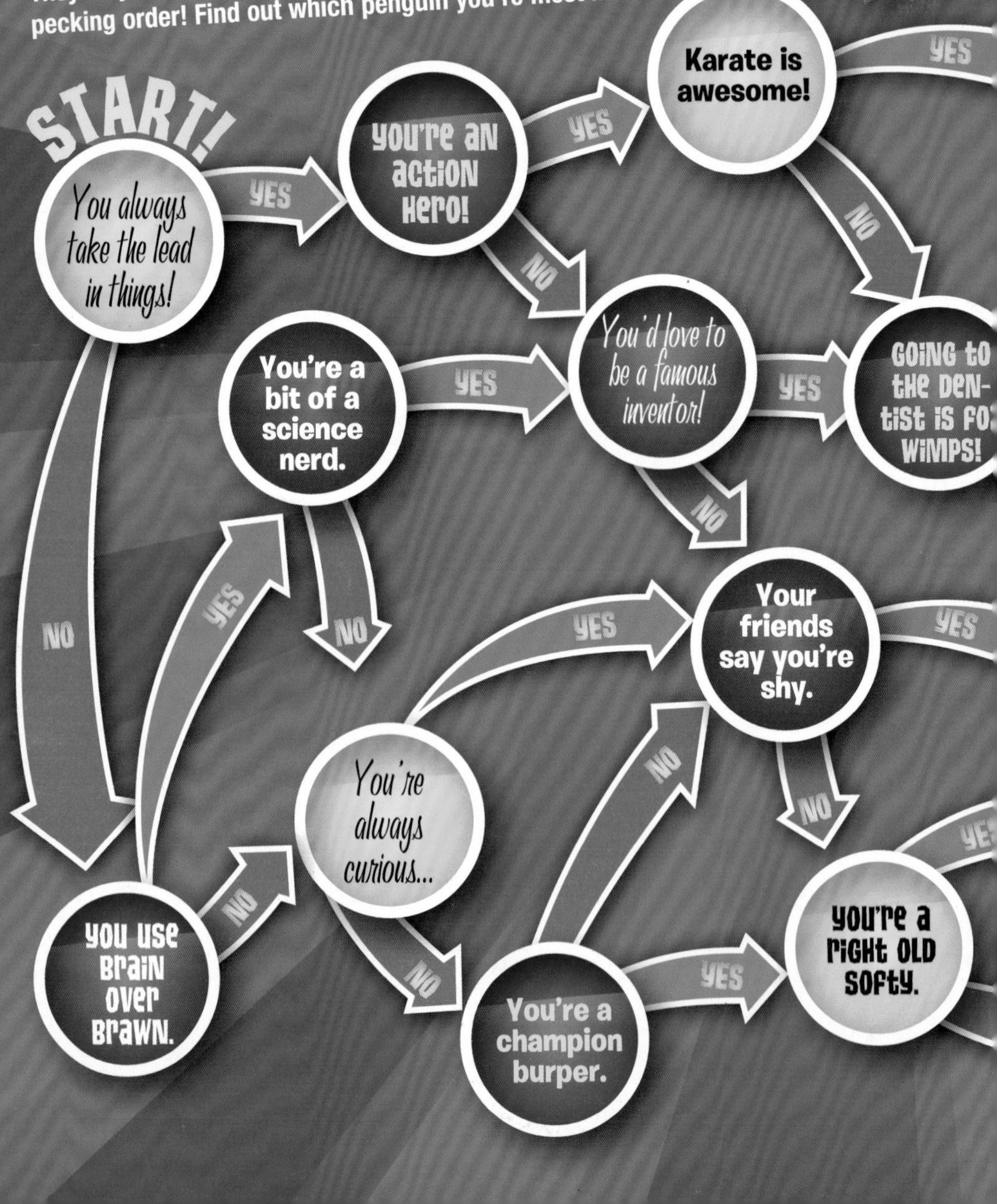
START!
You always take the lead in things!
YES
NO
You're an action hero!
YES
NO
Karate is awesome!
YES
NO
You're a bit of a science nerd.
YES
NO
You'd love to be a famous inventor!
YES
NO
Going to the dentist is fo
wimps!
Your friends say you're shy.
YES
NO
You use brain over brawn.
YES
NO
You're always curious...
YES
NO
You're a champion burper.
YES
NO
You're a right old softy.

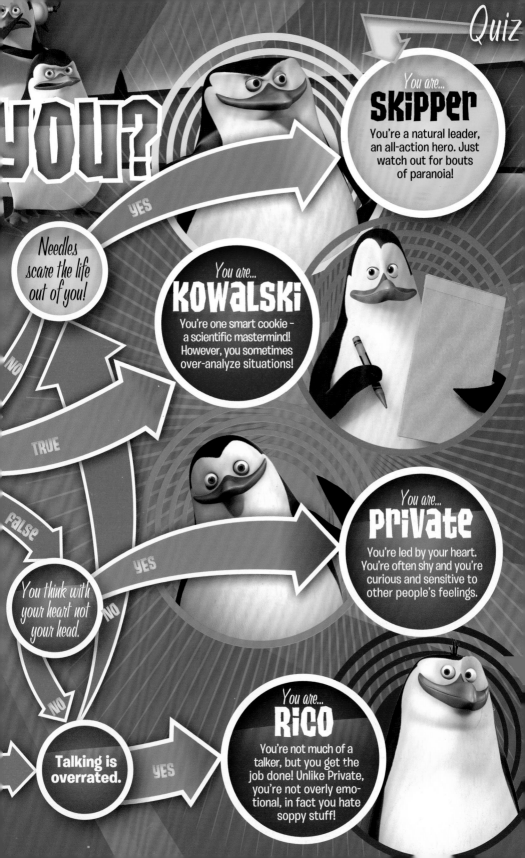

you?

YES

You are...
SKIPPER
You're a natural leader, an all-action hero. Just watch out for bouts of paranoia!

Needles scare the life out of you!

NO

You are...
KOWALSKI
You're one smart cookie – a scientific mastermind! However, you sometimes over-analyze situations!

TRUE

FALSE

YES

You are...
Private
You're led by your heart. You're often shy and you're curious and sensitive to other people's feelings.

You think with your heart not your head.

NO

NO

You are...
RICO
You're not much of a talker, but you get the job done! Unlike Private, you're not overly emotional, in fact you hate soppy stuff!

Talking is overrated.

YES

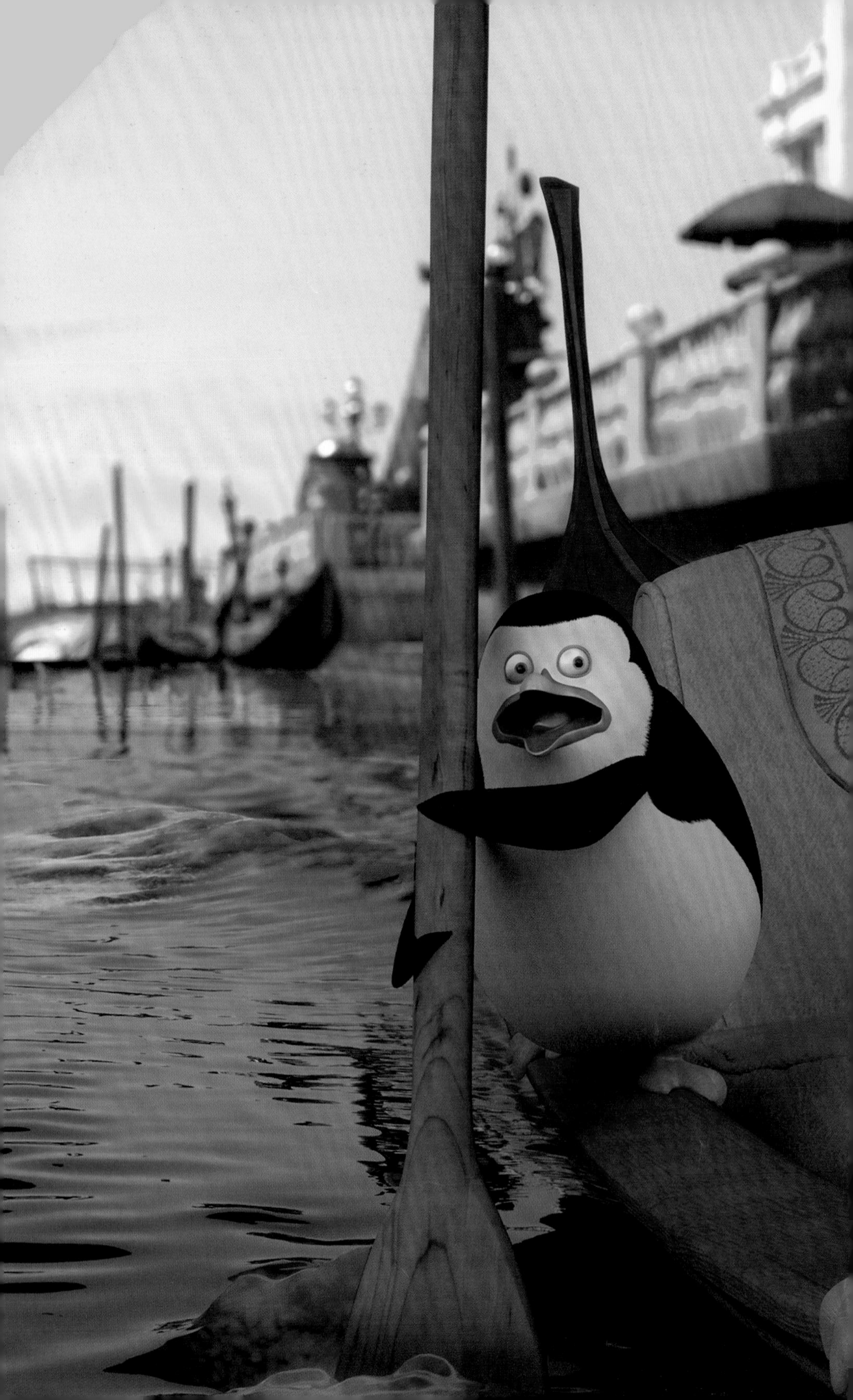

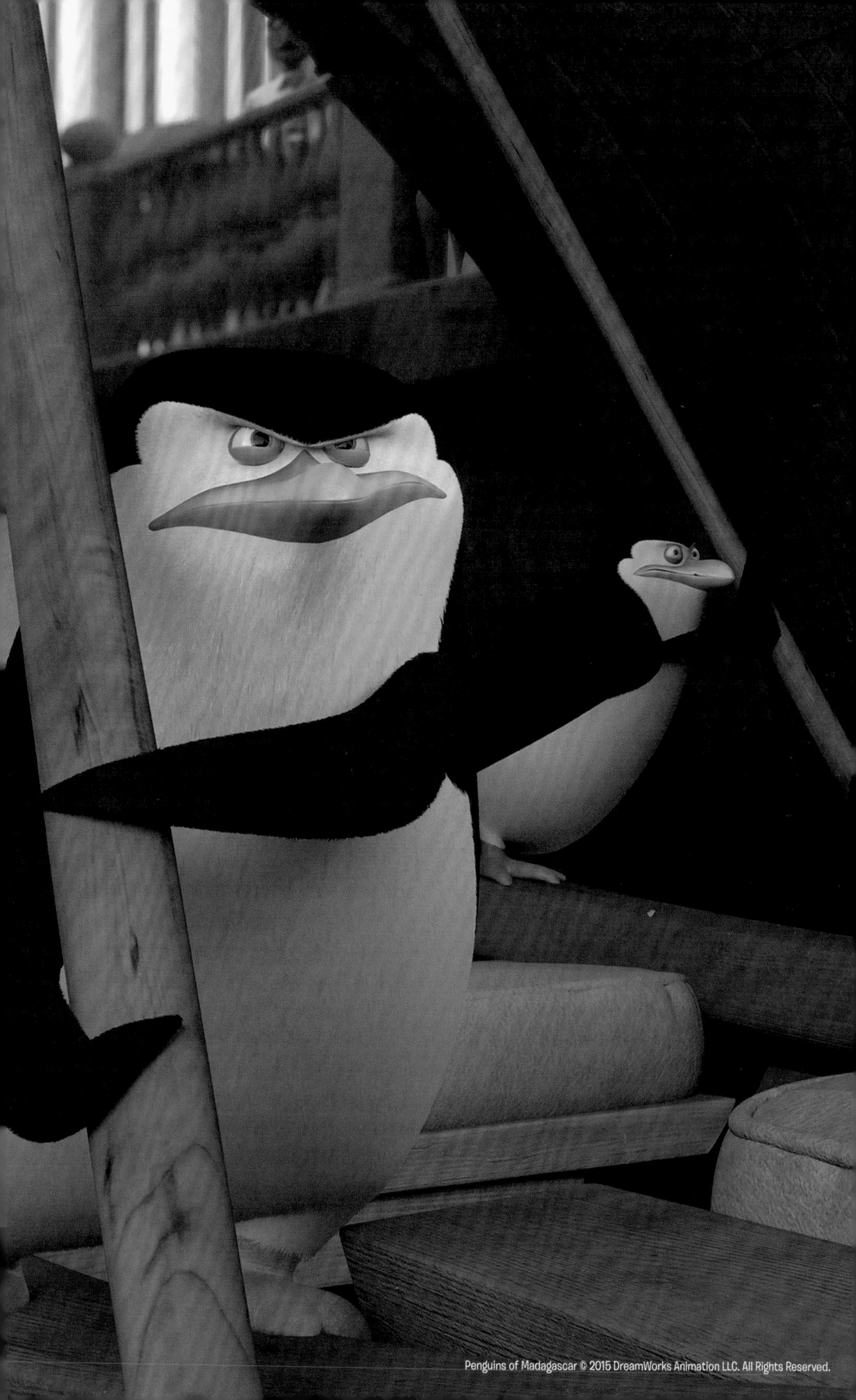

NIGHT OUT

SCRIPT
Dan Abnett & Andy Lanning

PENCILS
Anthony Williams

INKS
Dan Davis

COLORS
Robin Smith

LETTERING
Jimmy Betancourt/
Comicraft

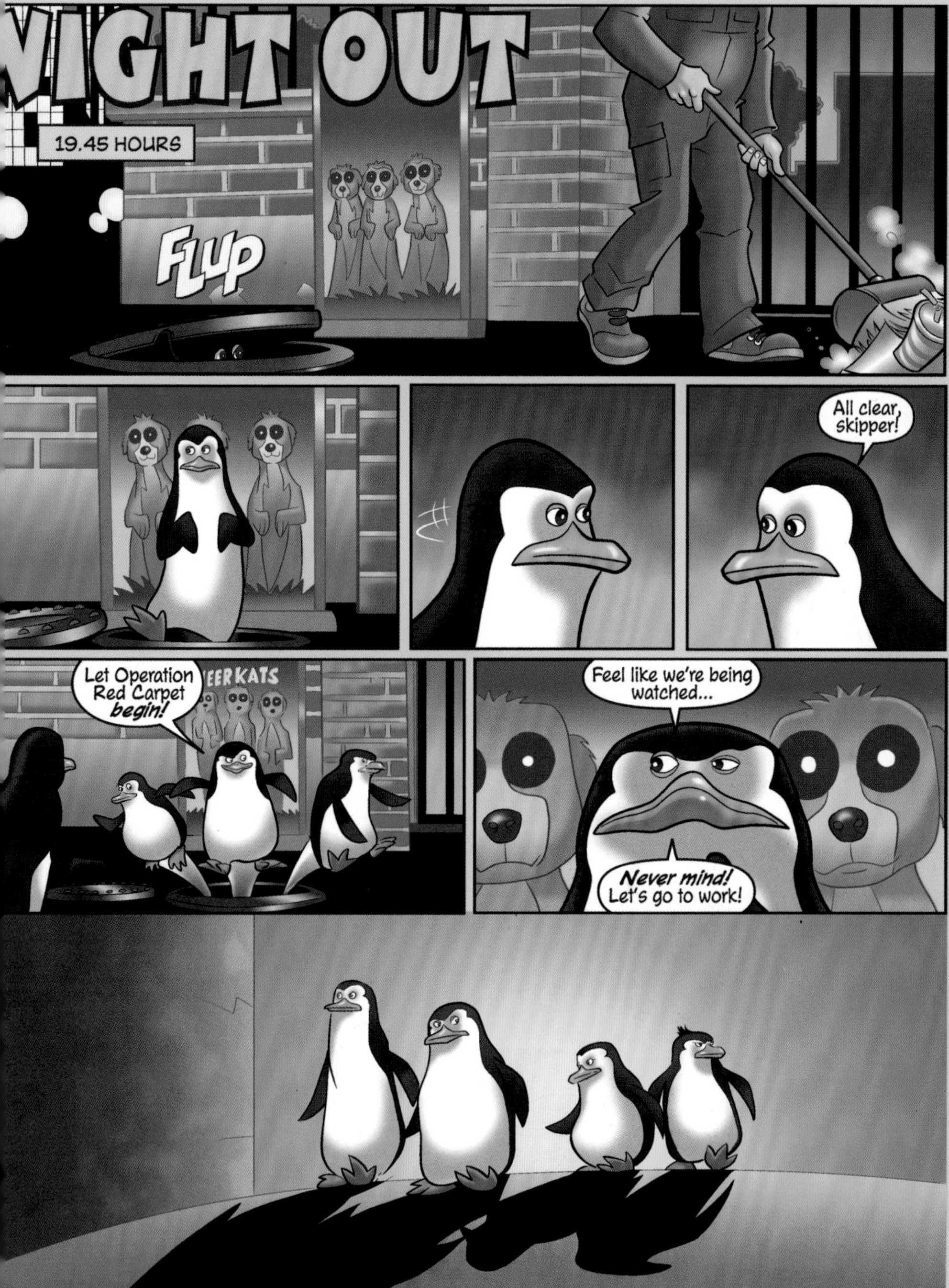
IGHT OUT
19.45 HOURS
FLUP
All clear, skipper!
Let Operation Red Carpet *begin!*
EER KATS
Feel like we're being watched...
Never mind! Let's go to work!

Okay, boys...

We need to be in position and locked down in the next five minutes!

Kowalski! Sit-rep!

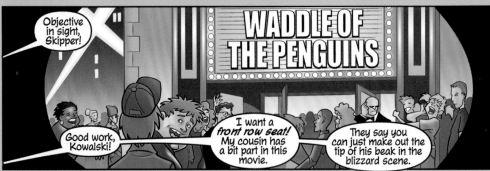

Objective in sight, Skipper!

WADDLE OF THE PENGUINS

Good work, Kowalski!

I want a *front row seat!* My cousin has a bit part in this movie.

They say you can just make out the tip of his beak in the blizzard scene.

Easy does it, boys...

Hey, dudes. Dig the costumes.

Just smile and wave, boys, smile and wave.

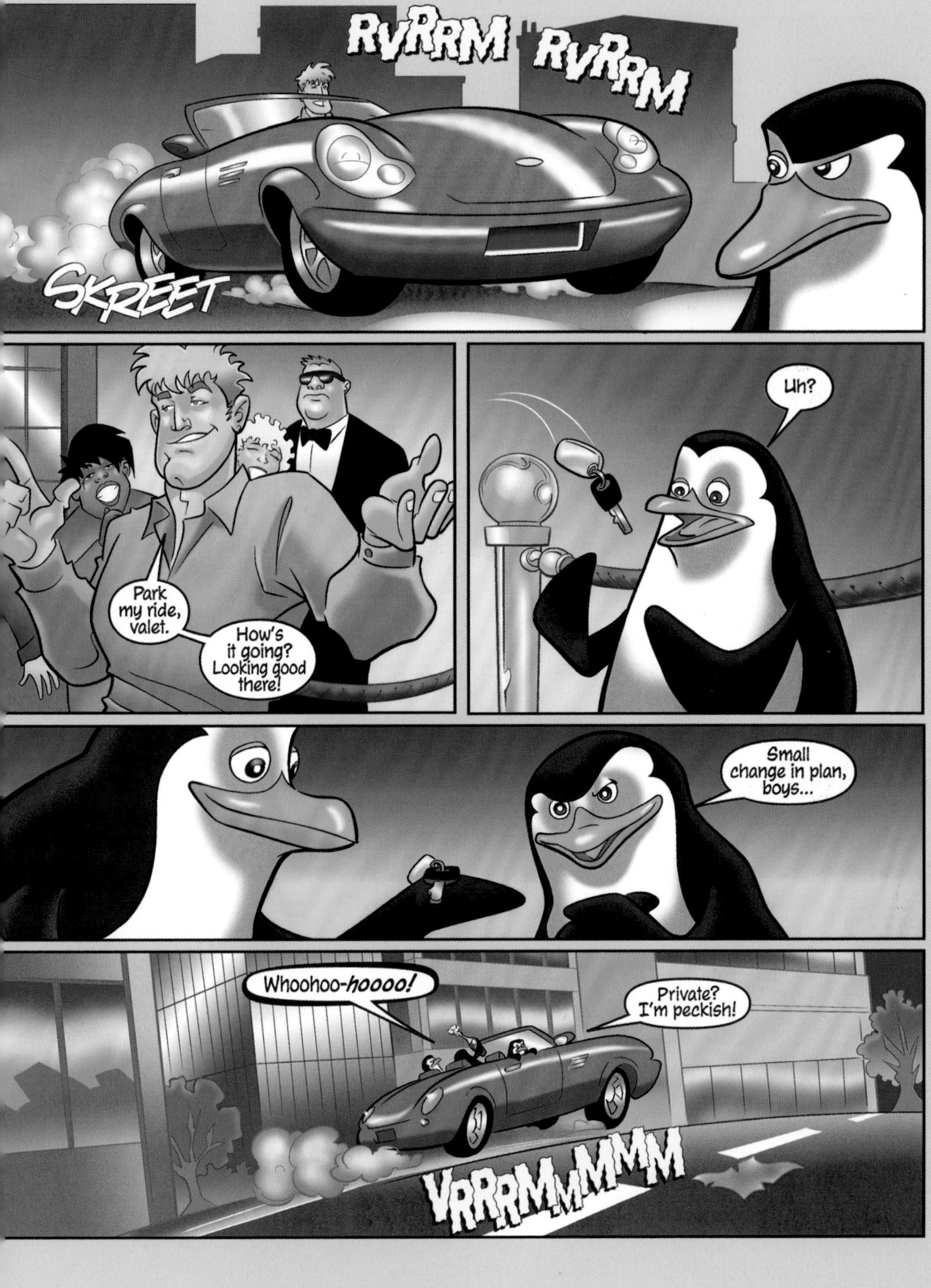
RVRRM RVRRM
SKREET
Park my ride, valet.
How's it going? Looking good there!
Uh?
Small change in plan, boys...
Whoohoo-hoooo!
Private? I'm peckish!
VRRRMMMMM

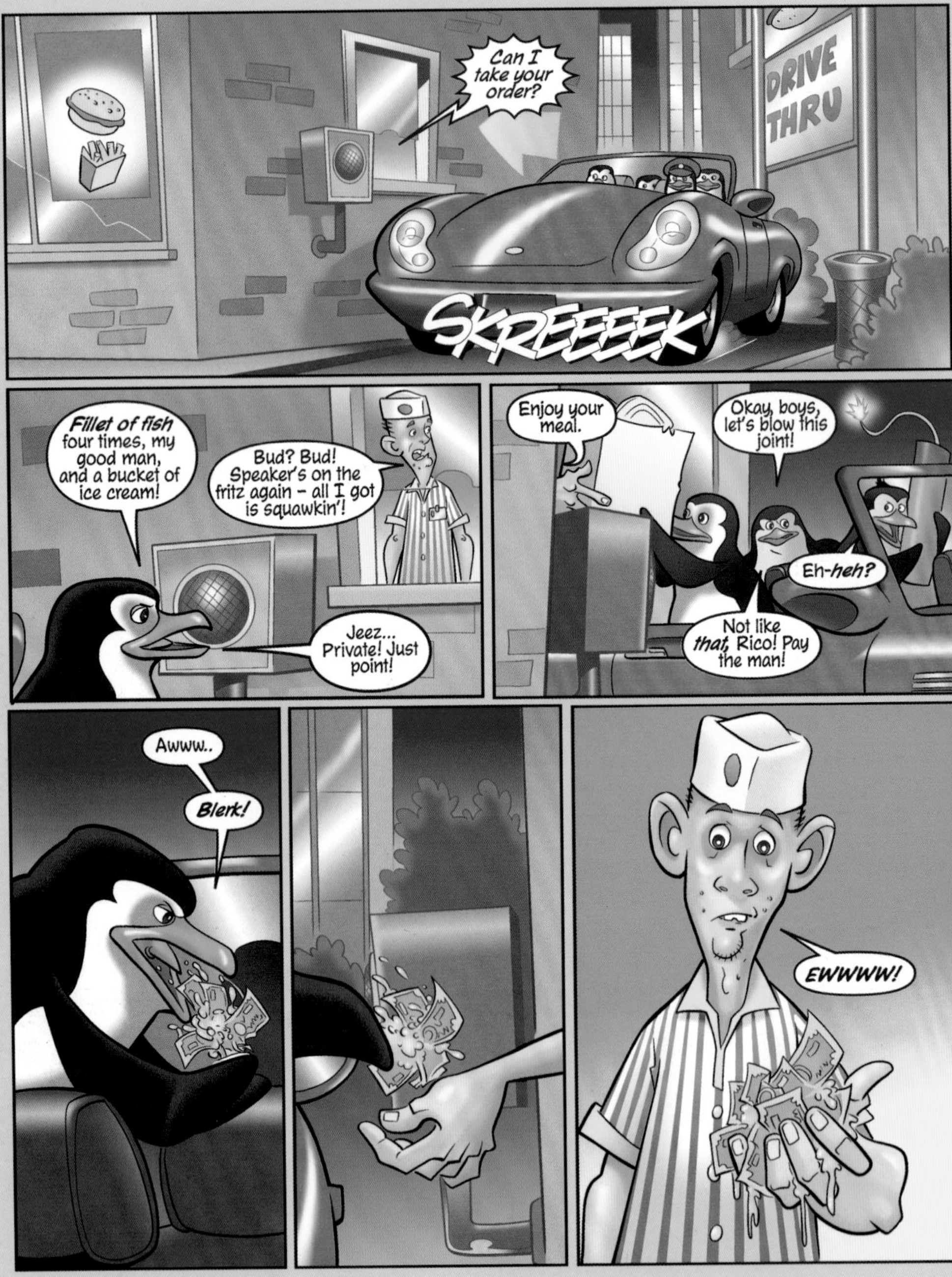
Can I take your order?
SKREEEEK
DRIVE THRU
Fillet of fish four times, my good man, and a bucket of ice cream!
Bud? Bud! Speaker's on the fritz again – all I got is squawkin'!
Jeez... Private! Just point!
Enjoy your meal.
Okay, boys, let's blow this joint!
Eh-heh?
Not like that, Rico! Pay the man!
Awww..
Blerk!
EWWWW!

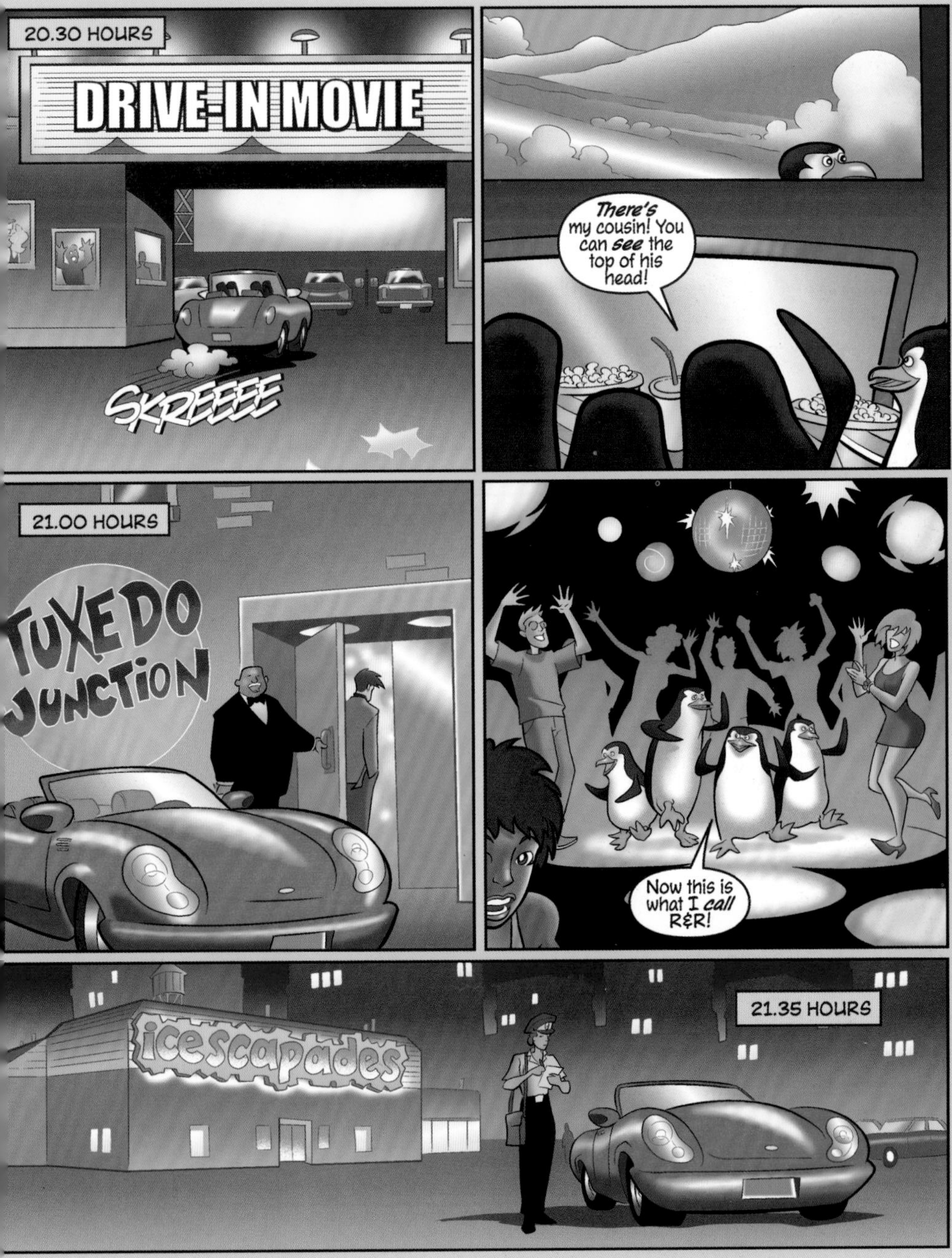
20.30 HOURS
DRIVE-IN MOVIE
SKREEEEE
There's my cousin! You can see the top of his head!
21.00 HOURS
TUXEDO JUNCTION
Now this is what I call R&R!
icescapades
21.35 HOURS

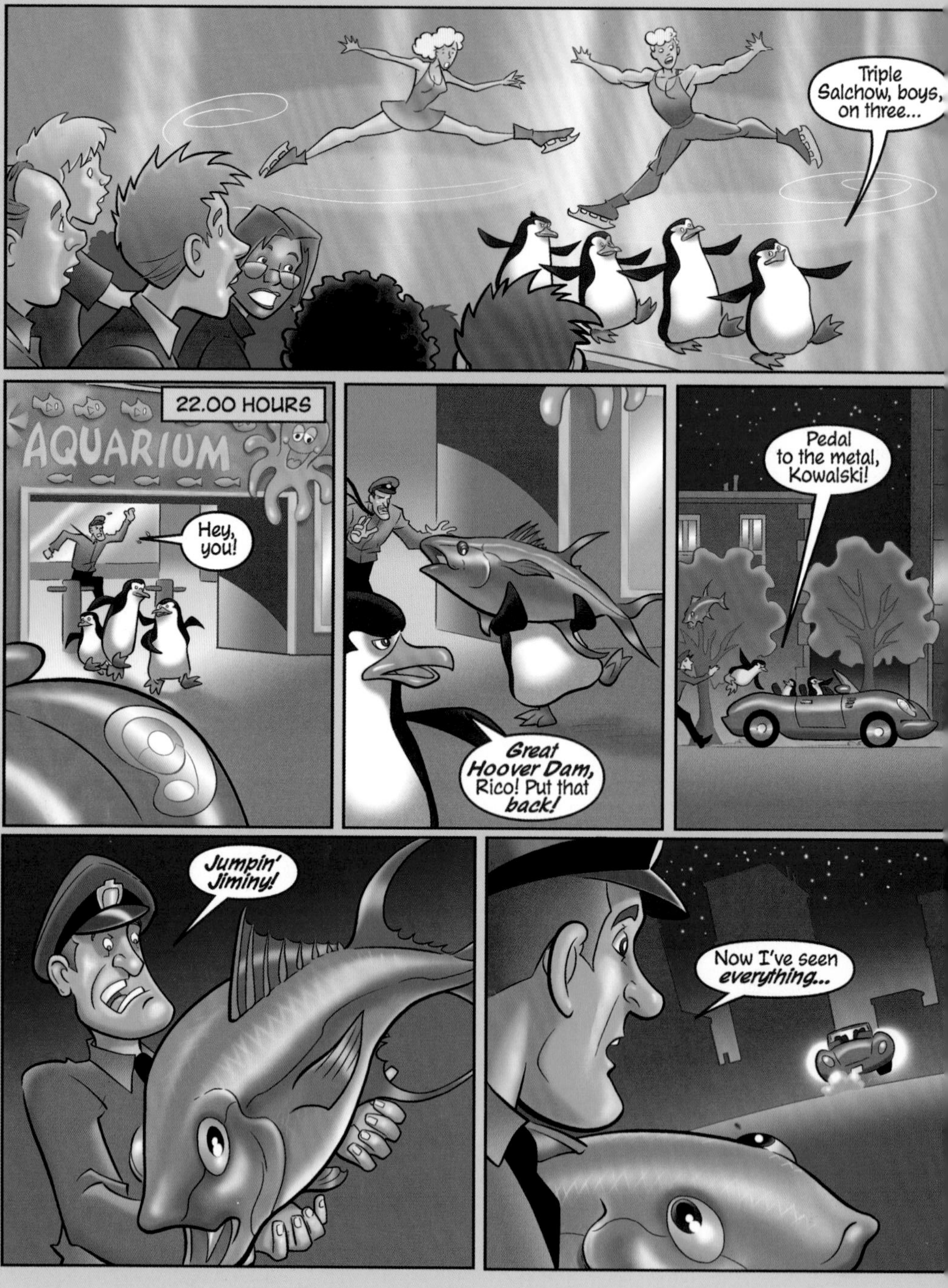
Triple Salchow, boys, on three...
22.00 HOURS
AQUARIUM
Hey, you!
Great Hoover Dam, Rico! Put that back!
Pedal to the metal, Kowalski!
Jumpin' Jiminy!
Now I've seen everything...

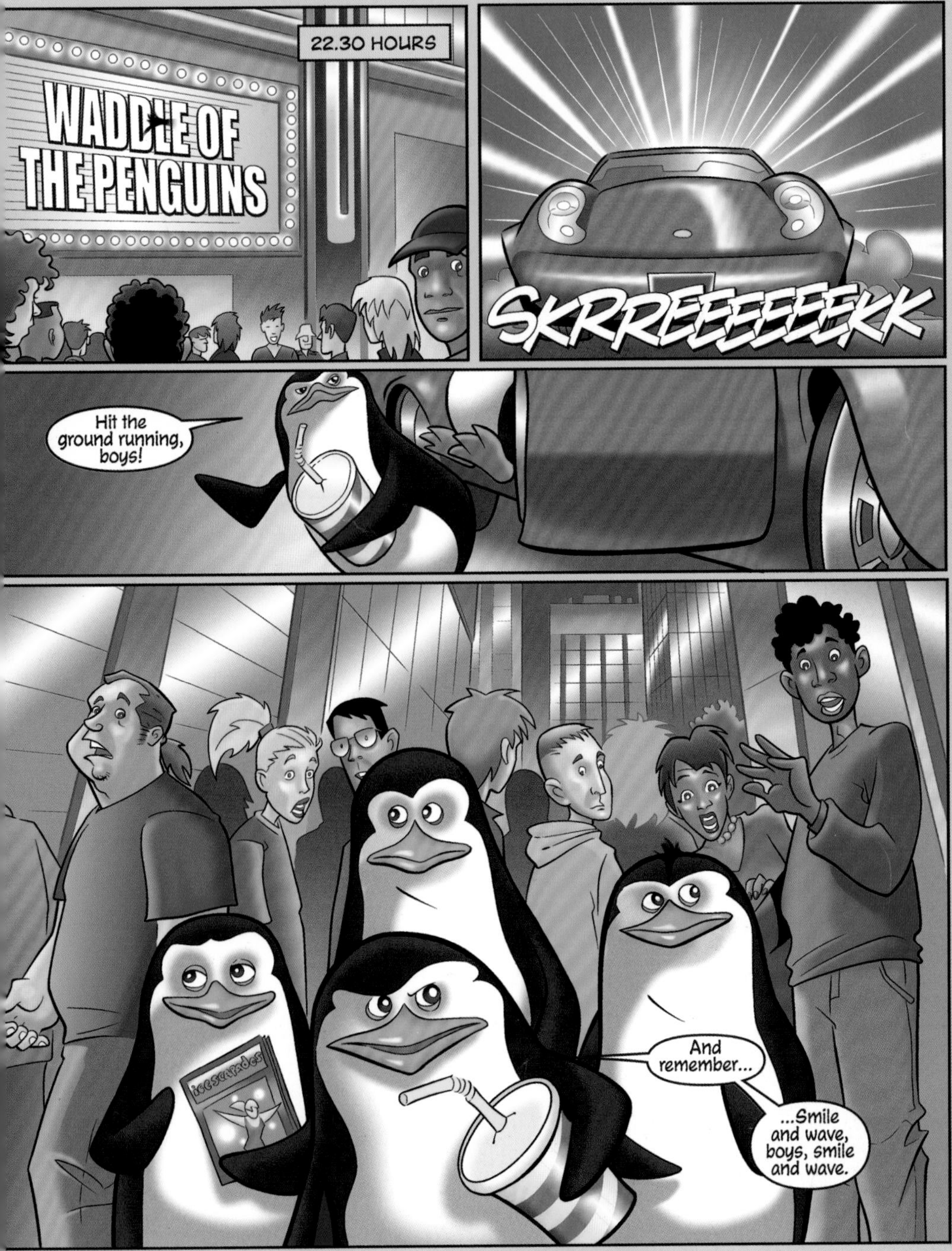
22.30 HOURS
WADDLE OF THE PENGUINS
SKRREEEEEEEKK
Hit the ground running, boys!
And remember...
...Smile and wave, boys, smile and wave.

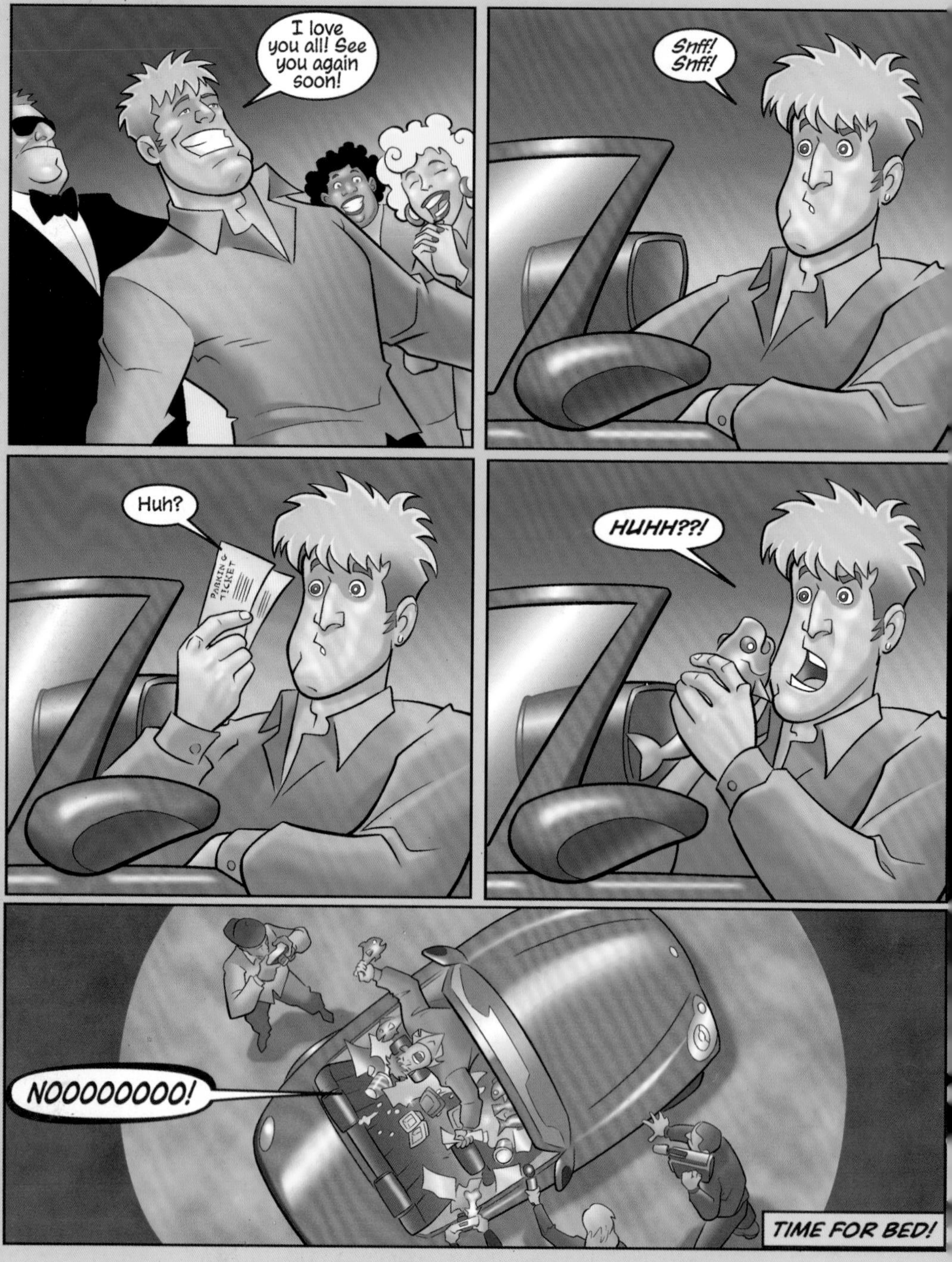
I love you all! See you again soon!
Snff! Snff!
Huh?
PARKING TICKET
HUHH??!
NOOOOOOOO!
TIME FOR BED!

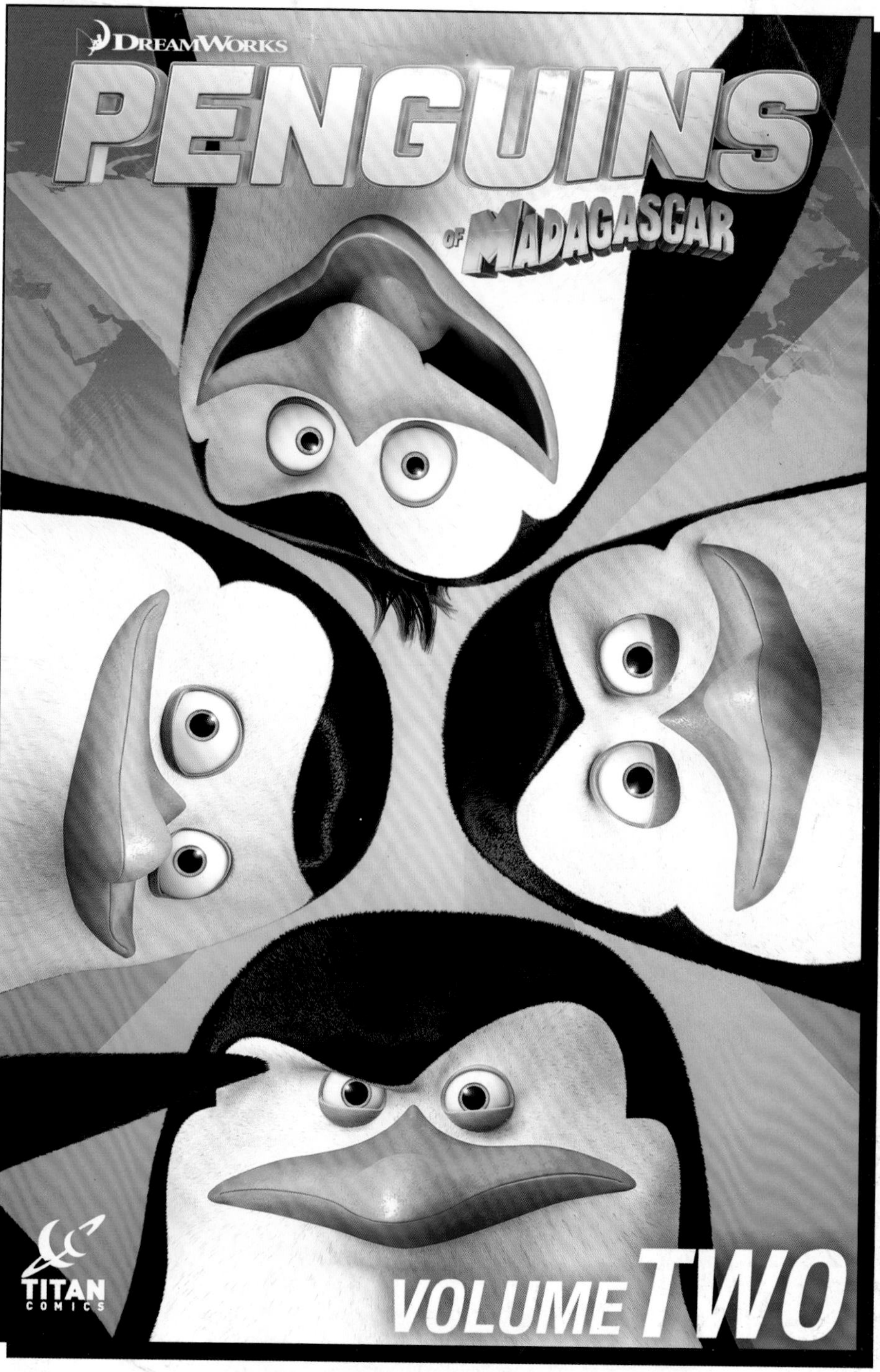
DreamWorks
PENGUINS
OF MADAGASCAR
TITAN COMICS
VOLUME TWO

DRAGONS
GRAPHIC NOVELS

VOLUME FOUR

OUT NOW $6.99

The Dragon Training Academy gets a new student —
a handsome, brave young man named Hroar. Hroar
becomes more and more popular by impressing
Hiccup's friends, but Hiccup grows increasingly
suspicious of him... Is Hroar hiding secrets...?

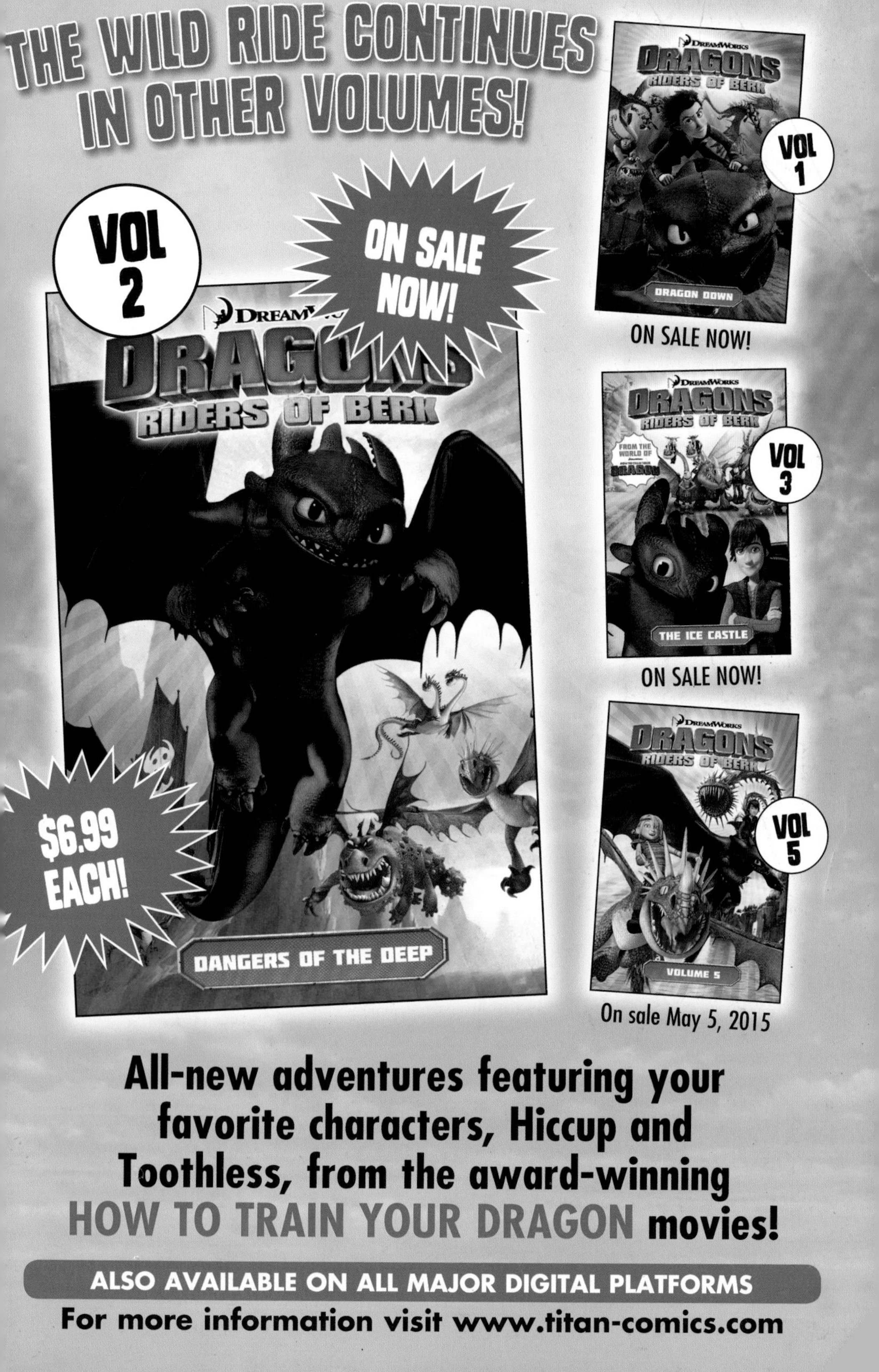
THE WILD RIDE CONTINUES IN OTHER VOLUMES!
VOL 2
ON SALE NOW!
DREAMWORKS DRAGONS RIDERS OF BERK
DANGERS OF THE DEEP
$6.99 EACH!
VOL 1
DREAMWORKS DRAGONS RIDERS OF BERK
DRAGON DOWN
ON SALE NOW!
VOL 3
DREAMWORKS DRAGONS RIDERS OF BERK
THE ICE CASTLE
ON SALE NOW!
VOL 5
DREAMWORKS DRAGONS RIDERS OF BERK
VOLUME 5
On sale May 5, 2015
All-new adventures featuring your favorite characters, Hiccup and Toothless, from the award-winning HOW TO TRAIN YOUR DRAGON movies!
ALSO AVAILABLE ON ALL MAJOR DIGITAL PLATFORMS
For more information visit www.titan-comics.com